GETTING

Rhonda Nelson

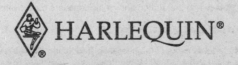

HARLEQUIN®

TORONTO • NEW YORK • LONDON
AMSTERDAM • PARIS • SYDNEY • HAMBURG
STOCKHOLM • ATHENS • TOKYO • MILAN • MADRID
PRAGUE • WARSAW • BUDAPEST • AUCKLAND

ISBN 0-373-79176-3

GETTING IT GOOD!

Copyright © 2005 by Rhonda Nelson.

This edition published by arrangement with Harlequin Books S.A.

® and TM are trademarks of the publisher. Trademarks indicated with
® are registered in the United States Patent and Trademark Office, the
Canadian Trade Marks Office and in other countries.

www.eHarlequin.com

Printed in U.S.A.

...ved a long-suffering sigh.
...always so arrogant?"

"That depends," Ross countered. "Are your nipples always so hard?"

She glanced at his crotch. "Are *you* always so hard?

Ross chuckled. He wasn't the least surprised by her candor, but he wasn't going to let her get off easily. In fact, he wasn't planning on letting her get off for a while.... He hauled her against him, rocked his pelvis forward and swiftly lowered his head, catching her surprised gasp with his mouth. "I am around you, Frankie," he admitted with a resigned laugh. "Always around you."

Then he nudged her forward, ending the moment. "But right now, Carnal Contessa, our fans are waiting for our advice. So move your ass, dearest."

Their public wanted heat, Ross thought. Fine, he'd give them some heat. And by the time this session was finished, he'd make sure that nothing but ashes remained of the doubts Frankie *pretended* to have about the authenticity of their attraction.

Playtime was over. It was time for truth or consequences.

Blaze™

Dear Reader,

Welcome back to my CHICKS IN CHARGE series! (If you missed *Getting It!* last month in Harlequin Temptation, be sure to check out eHarlequin for a new copy. You won't want to miss it.) To say that I'm enjoying this group of feisty women—and finding their perfect heroes—would be a huge understatement.

Card-carrying member of CHICKS IN CHARGE Frankie Salvaterra is the Carnal Contessa of the up-and-coming magazine—CHiCs. She's the resident *sexpert*, and her plain speaking and outrageous suggestions for spicing up a flavorless sex life have quickly propelled her to semistardom. But when a meddling matchmaking friend steps in, Frankie finds herself sharing a room with CHiC's newest employee— The Duke of Desire, Ross Hartford. Too-sexy Ross is every bit as outrageous as she is, every bit as confident when it comes to bed play—a lethal combination, to be sure. When Ross and Frankie are thrust into a royal "He Said, She Said" promotional tour for the magazine, Frankie finds it harder and harder to hang on to her righteous indignation...particularly since she'd rather hold on to him.

Be sure to look for my first single title release, *The Future Widows' Club,* coming to Harlequin Signature Spotlight in April. Also, I love to hear from my readers, so swing by my Web site— www.booksbyRhondaNelson.com—and sign my guest book.

Enjoy!

Rhonda Nelson

Books by Rhonda Nelson

HARLEQUIN BLAZE
 75—JUST TOYING AROUND
 81—SHOW & TELL
115—PICTURE ME SEXY
140—THE SEX DIET
158—1-900-LOVER

HARLEQUIN TEMPTATION
 973—UNFORGETTABLE
1007—GETTING IT!

Dear Reader,

An Evening To Remember... Those words evoke all kinds of emotions and memories. How do you plan a romantic evening with your guy that will help you get in touch with each other on every level?

Start with a great dinner that you cook together. Be sure to light several candles and put fresh flowers on the table. Enjoy a few glasses of wine and pick out your favorite music to set the mood. After dinner take the time to really talk to each other. Hold hands and snuggle on the sofa in front of the fireplace. And maybe take a few minutes to read aloud selected sexy scenes from your favorite Harlequin Blaze novel. After that, anything can happen....

That's just one way to have an evening to remember. There are so many more. Write and tell us how you keep the spark in your relationship. And don't forget to check out our Web site at www.eHarlequin.com.

Sincerely,

Birgit Davis-Todd
Executive Editor

Though the dedication is the only part of this book she can read until she's much older, this book is lovingly dedicated to my darling daughter, Allie. You're the best, *ma petite amie*. I'm growing my very own best friend. How cool is that?

Prologue

The Bet

"I'LL SEE YOUR MASSAGE and raise you a blow job."

A slow, wicked smile curved Tate Hatcher's mouth. "Confident, are you?"

Zora slid the customized fellatio chip to the center of the table and gave her husband a small enigmatic smile. *Horny* better described her current state, but let him think what he would.

She wasn't a great poker player and, to make matters worse, when she and Tate played Dirty Poker she always seemed to be the first player to lose focus. Her gaze skimmed over him. But who wouldn't, with a husband as sexy as hers? Her nerve endings tingled with needy anticipation and a slow steady throb commenced between her thighs. Hell, she was tempted to fold simply to get the game over with.

But she couldn't.

At least, not yet. She'd been waiting for months for a hand like this and, though he didn't know it, she intended to up the ante in an unexpected way very soon.

Tate blew out a breath and those aged-whiskey eyes shrewdly considered her. "I think you're bluffing… But on the off chance that you're not, I'm going to see your blow job—" he dropped another fellatio chip into the growing pile and lowered his voice "—and raise you a secret fantasy."

Zora arched a brow and thoughtfully tapped her cards. A secret fantasy, eh? Tate was a conservative player, didn't raise the stakes unless he was confident of the outcome, therefore one could reasonably assume that he had one helluva hand.

With effort, she suppressed a small smile. Even a helluva hand wasn't going to beat the one she currently held. The odds that he had the only hand that would beat it were too slim. Out of the realm of true possibility.

In other words, she had him.

Though every nerve tingled with excited energy, Zora pretended to consider her cards once more, then let her gaze tangle with his. She cocked her head. "Why don't we make this a little more interesting?"

Tate's eyes instantly sparkled with smoky arousal. "Oh? How so?"

She leaned forward. "Let's forget Dirty Poker for the moment and talk about matchmaking between a couple of mutual friends."

The abrupt change in subject matter cleared the heat from his gaze. Tate heaved a long-suffering sigh and simultaneously slouched back in his seat. "Zora, do we honestly have to have this conversation again? We shouldn't meddle. It's rude."

"It's only rude if we're wrong. And we're not. You know they're perfect for each other." An argument she'd presented for months, yet Tate still firmly refused to "meddle."

"No, I don't. I *suspect* that they would suit. However, I don't *know* and, more to the point, neither do you." He paused. "Jesus. They can't be in a room together without verbal bloodshed."

That was true, Zora had to concur. Frankie

Salvaterra and Ross Hartford seemed to dislike each other simply for the pure sport of it. Though they both claimed to detest the other, they nevertheless never missed an opportunity to argue or disagree. One would think that where so much animosity existed, they would both go out of their way to avoid the other—and yet, curiously, they didn't. In fact, Zora suspected they secretly enjoyed their little battles and she further suspected that there was an underlying reason for their exaggerated aversion—intense sexual attraction. The very air around them seemed to vibrate with it, shimmery and warm. Hell, *she* could feel it.

Tate gave his head an uncertain shake and winced. "It would never work, Zora. They're like oil and water."

"Or oil and gasoline," she countered, more convinced than ever that she was right. After all, that's what everyone had thought about them, too. Tate had been the bane of her existence, a thorn in her side, had crashed her first *Chicks-In-Charge* conference, intent on gathering unflattering book fodder for his next release…and she'd ended up marrying him. What had been the odds of that? That they'd ever suit? And yet she loved him more with each passing day. Zora let go a sigh. "I think you're wrong, and if I win this hand, then you have to help me set them up."

He groaned. "That's what you meant by 'let's make it interesting'?"

She nodded. "Yep."

Tate glanced idly at his cards and something about that careless regard made her inexplicably nervous. "And what do I get if I win?"

Since there was no way she could possibly lose this hand, Zora hadn't considered what she'd offer in return. But she'd indulge him. She smiled, lowered her voice, and let her gaze purposefully drop to his mouth. "What do you want?"

Tate was silent for the better part of a minute, then a slow calculating grin that made the fine hairs on her arms stand on end spread across his too handsome face. "I want you to hire Ross, let him come to work at *Chicks-In-Charge*."

"*What?*"

Tate nodded, clearly pleased with his choice. And no wonder. As founder of *Chicks-In-*

Charge—a national organization designed expressly for the purpose of empowering women—Zora was adamantly opposed to hiring men for any of her ventures. Sexist? Yes. But she'd been burned very badly by a former boyfriend/boss—which was how *Chicks-In-Charge* had gotten its start in the first place—and so far the concept had worked very well for her. She provided a completely testosterone-free workplace and all of her employees loved it.

Zora frowned thoughtfully. Particularly Frankie, who'd been scorched pretty badly by her father. "You know I can't do that," Zora finally said, mildly irritated. Hell, she'd compromised her principles enough by getting married. *Hire a man?* No way. "Besides, he has a job. He wouldn't take it."

"Oh, I can guarantee that he would take it." An evil sort of glee clung to his smile. "If he wants the Maxwell account he'll take it." Tate's advertising firm held the prestigious honor of catering to many of the larger men's market accounts, and the Maxwell account was an especially juicy plum.

Zora gasped. "Tate, that's horrible." And, yet

so diabolical she found it sexy. "Hadn't you planned on giving him that account anyway?"

Smiling, he nodded. "Yeah…but he doesn't know that. Besides, it would be worth it to see you add a man to your payroll." He shifted in his seat, looked heavenward and heaved a dramatic sigh. *"God, would it ever be worth it."*

"You know I can't do that," Zora replied tightly. "Pick something else. Anything else."

"Nope. That's what I want," he insisted, to Zora's supreme irritation. He thoughtfully considered her once more and one side of his mouth kicked up in a faintly smug smile. "Guess you're not as confident as I thought you were. That, or you just don't want this bad enough."

Though she knew better than to react, the somewhat mocking taunt overrode her initial hesitation. "Oh, I'm confident, and I most definitely want this." Frankie needed someone. Desperately. And Zora simply knew—*knew*—that Ross was the man for her. Besides, there was simply no way Tate could beat her hand. The odds were too great against it. Still, if hell froze over and she did lose this hand, then it would be better to have set a few conditions and parameters. "Temporary employment?"

"Define 'temporary.'"

"An hour."

Tate laughed. "Not long enough. Try a month."

"In your dreams. A week tops," Zora countered.

He nodded succinctly. "Done. What have you got?"

Now, for the moment of truth. Zora grinned and carefully spread her hand down on the table. "I've got a straight flush, baby. Read 'em and weep." She threw her head back and a giddy burst of triumphant laughter bubbled up her throat.

Tate hummed under his breath and his head bobbed a single nod of agreement. "That is a good hand," he conceded lightly. "But mine's better—"

Zora's gleeful chortling came to an abrupt halt and the smile slid from her face. *"What?"*

"—because I've got a *royal* flush." Tate laid his cards down on the table.

Stunned, Zora shook her head. Dread curdled

in her stomach. "No," she said faintly. "But you can't— I— It's not possible."

He smiled. "Oh, but it is." He cheerfully slid the pot from the middle of the table. "So, what do I want first?" Tate pondered aloud with the exaggerated air of a child who'd just been told Christmas had come early this year. "Do I want a massage? A blow job? A secret fantasy?" His eyes twinkled with evil humor. "Or do I want you to call Ross *right now* and offer him a job at the magazine?" He pretended to think about it for a couple of seconds, then nodded dramatically. "Yeah. That's what I want. I want you to call Ross. Right now." Then to Zora's immense irritation, he howled with laughter.

"If you're going to have to blackmail him into taking the position shouldn't I wait until we can both talk to him?"

Still laughing, Tate shook his head. "No."

A frustrated growl vibrated the back of Zora's throat. "Dammit, Tate, I don't even know what I'm going to hire him to do, for pity's sake."

God, what *was* she going to hire him to do? Zora wondered with mounting alarm. There were no current openings, she was fully staffed at *CHiC,* her web-based e-zine, which had just made its debut into a glossy format. Furthermore, since it looked like she would definitely have to add Ross to the payroll—albeit only for a week—she should definitely make the most of it by putting Ross and Frankie in close proximity. Which would be next to impossible because Frankie—*CHiC's* resident sexpert, the Carnal Contessa—would be on tour promoting the new glossy format the magazine had recently adopted.

Zora paused as a flush of inspiration suddenly lessened the panic crowding her brain. Wait a minute. This could actually work to her advantage. *What if...* A slow smile worked its way across her lips. *Oh, God. That was perfect.* Tate had not specified in what capacity she had to hire Ross, just simply that she must.

Tate's laughter trailed off and ended with a deep satisfied sigh. He glanced at her, then frowned. "Why are you smiling?" he asked warily. "I won. I'm the one who's smiling. Not you. You're not supposed to smile. You're supposed to worry and fret and eat humble pie. This is supposed to be a character lesson, a crash course in the benefit of humility."

Zora grinned. "Whatever."

"Whatever? What do you mean whatever?" His eyes narrowed. "Just what exactly have you got up your sleeve?"

"You'll see," Zora replied mysteriously. "Right now, however, I believe I have a few plans to make."

1

FRANKIE SALVATERRA inhaled sharply. *"You've hired the Antichrist?"*

Zora's lips curled into a droll smile. "A wee bit dramatic, don't you think? God, it's stifling in here." She threw open the French doors behind her desk, allowing the crisp New Orleans autumn air to drift inside. "And I haven't hired him yet—but I did offer him a job."

"A job?" Frankie repeated incredulously. "Here? At *CHiC?*"

Her current boss and *former* best friend sat, then leaned back in her padded executive chair. She nodded once. "Yes, here. With you, specifically. But," she sighed, "it's only temporary and, though I've been assured that he'll take it, there is still the chance that he won't."

With her? Frankie thought ominously. No,

Zora couldn't be serious, had to be joking. She couldn't work with Ross. He was a stubborn, arrogant ass with an exalted opinion of his wit. He breathed to annoy her. She abhorred him, detested him. And yet, despite all of that, there was a small part of her which she refused to consciously acknowledge that was utterly captivated by him.

Ross Hartford was one of those fix-me males, the sexy-as-hell, rough-around-the-edges, you're-the-only-woman-who-can-tame-me kind of guys that Frankie was inherently—stupidly— attracted to. His face was a masterpiece of masculine planes and angles—sinfully high cheekbones, dramatically hollow cheeks, a strong angular jaw and a sexy dimpled cleft that she'd fantasized about tasting one too many times. He had light brown tousled locks, eyes that were neither green nor blue nor hazel, but a compelling combination of all three, a voice that was low and smooth and a mouth that made her wet even when it curled into a mocking grin.

Which was beyond intolerable and only increased her desire to hate him.

Muttering a string of obscenities, Frankie

vaulted from her seat and paced the plush office. She simply couldn't believe this. Could *not* believe it. She'd known Zora Anderson-Hatcher since college, had been right there with her when the concept for *Chicks-In-Charge* had been born and had heard her say on countless occasions that she'd *never* hire a man. It was no small part of the reason Frankie loved working for *CHiC,* why she'd been drawn to and ultimately proud of being a part of the *Chicks-In-Charge* organization.

And despite that vehement credo, Zora'd not only abandoned it altogether, but hired the worst possible man on the damned planet and had the further effrontery to pair her with him?

She frowned, then irritably rubbed the line from between her brows. It just didn't make any sense. Was completely out of character. Totally rash. What on earth had possessed her to—

Frankie gasped and whirled to face her. "You've been playing Dirty Poker again, haven't you?"

Her boss flushed guiltily and looked away.

"Zora," Frankie all but wailed, outraged. "You're a terrible poker player! You rarely win.

How could you bet something like this?" Irritation and disgust propelled her back into her chair. She shook her head, shoved a handful of hair behind her ear. "I can't believe you did this! What on earth were you thinking?"

Zora huffed a despondent sigh, rolled her eyes. "I was thinking that I'd win, that's what I was thinking. I had a straight flush."

Intrigued, Frankie glanced up. "A straight flush? Then how did you—"

She smirked. "Tate had a *royal* flush."

"Oh." Well, that sucked. Nevertheless... "So what did you bet? That you'd hire a man, or that you'd hire Ross?" Frankie grimly suspected that she knew the answer, but hope prompted her to ask the question anyway.

Zora winced. "Ross. But it's only for a week, and like I said, he may not take the job."

Frankie scowled. This still didn't make any sense. "Fine," she conceded with an impatient wave of her hand. "You have to hire him for a week. That still doesn't explain why he has to work with me."

Zora hesitated, then steepled her fingers beneath her chin. "Don't take this the wrong way…but to be totally frank, I'm making him work with you because I know he'll hate it." Eyes narrowed, her lips slid into a determinedly grim smile. "If he has to work here, he's *not* going to like it."

Frankie found herself conflicted. Since she couldn't stand Ross, anything that he found unpleasant or made him unhappy appealed to her, and being the author of his misery would ordinarily tickle her to death, but for reasons she didn't understand, something about Zora casting her in the role was somewhat…depressing. Her shoulders sagged marginally.

Everyone was supposed to notice that *she* couldn't stand *him,* not the other way around, dammit. *He* should be grateful to share the same air as her.

An arrogant, exaggerated opinion, but she couldn't help herself. Every emotion she had pertaining to Ross Hartford felt…exaggerated. Magnified. There were lots of men who got on her nerves, but she didn't look forward to verbally eviscerating them. Lots of men she found attractive, but she didn't constantly—graphically—dream and fantasize about them.

In fact, as a species in general, Frankie didn't have any use for men at all. In her experience they were all untrustworthy, thoughtless, scheming, dick-driven bastards—and her father had been the worst of the lot.

Frankie had worked her ass off for the cheating SOB for eight years—had started with the company when she'd only been sixteen—and rather than give her the VP promotion she'd not only earned, but would have been handed to a male heir, he'd given *her* job to the Bagel Girl. Frankie's lips twisted with bitter humor.

Turned out that she'd been giving him more than a little extra cream cheese every morning when she'd made her way around the office—she'd been giving him a nooner before noon.

That or the whore simply couldn't tell time.

Frankie let go a frustrated, disgusted breath. How her mother could justify staying with him absolutely mind-boggled her. She'd never understand it. Never.

Between her rotten excuse for a father and one serious-but-soured relationship, Frankie had adopted only one attitude from her male counterparts that she found useful—indifference.

When she desired companionship, she hung out with female friends. When she wanted sex, she took an occasional lover. Things were less complicated that way. The idea of a man being both a friend and a lover was completely foreign to her. In order to call a person a friend, you had to trust them. Since she didn't trust any man, the whole *boyfriend* concept was simply a misnomer to her.

Granted Zora and Tate seemed to have made things work, but they seemed to be the exception to the rule. Her gaze inexplicably slid to their wedding photo proudly displayed on the credenza and she felt a rebellious twinge of envy prick her heart. Zora and Tate were clearly head-over-heels for each other, and Tate was obviously Zora's best friend.

Regardless, Frankie would rather rock along on her own than put a toe out of her comfort zone and she'd be damned before she'd ever let a man make a fool of her. She'd never allow herself to love someone so much that she'd give up her self-respect. The image of her mother's rigid but weary form posted by the window waiting on her lousy father to come home flashed through her mind, punctuating the thought.

Besides, she *liked* her life. There was a lot to be said for peace of mind, for ultimate remote-control power, for hogging the whole bed, for doing *what* she wanted *when* she wanted without having to consider anyone else's feelings. It was a very liberated if sometimes lonely lifestyle.

Furthermore, she loved her job. She'd found her niche as *CHiC's* Carnal Contessa. Empowering women through sexuality was a noble goal. Teaching them to voice their needs, to act upon their baser desires, to be confident in their femininity, and more often than not, telling them to advise their blockheaded lovers on how to please them, was rewarding work. In her bi-weekly column, she leavened her sassy, blunt advice with a healthy lump of humor, and so far, the combination had worked beautifully.

So well, in fact, that beginning next week she'd start a five-city tour across the U.S. promoting the new glossy format of the magazine. She'd been honored that Zora had asked her to do it, and really looked forward to promoting *CHiC* and the whole *Chicks-In-Charge* movement. Both had really changed her life and she desperately wanted to give something back, wanted to share the phenomenon with other women.

Frankie paused. Since she wouldn't be in the office, would be on tour, just exactly how was Ross supposed to work with her over the next week? The hair on her nape prickled and a cold knot of dread formed in her suddenly roiling tummy.

She carefully looked up. "Zora, just exactly—"

"If he takes the job, he'll be going with you," Zora said, anticipating her question.

Frankie swallowed the urge to scream and puke at once. "With me? As what? My assistant?" She hesitated, a sudden image popping into her head. Ooh, this could work, she thought as the idea gained momentum. She'd love bossing him around, sending him on pointless errands, giving him degrading tasks designed expressly to turn his mind black with rage. A bolt of evil glee shot through her, but withered at the small shake of Zora's head.

"Nooo," she replied, dragging the word out. Then a wicked smile bloomed across her lips and her eyes twinkled with devilish humor. "He's going to be *CHiC's* temporary Duke of Desire."

Frankie frowned. Duke of Desire? But— A beat slid into three, then comprehension dawned and a low chuckle vibrated the back of her throat.

Equally impressed and awed, she returned Zora's grin. "Oh, he's going to hate that," she said with vengeful relish. "He's *really* going to hate it."

Zora nodded. "Precisely. Think you can suffer through it?"

Frankie nodded without hesitation. The mere idea of Ross's impending discomfort was balm enough for her battered ego. "Oh, yeah. I can suffer through it."

But she happily suspected he'd be suffering more.

"YOU'RE KIDDING," Ross chuckled, stunned. He snagged a cup of coffee from his beleaguered assistant along with the usual stack of morning messages and hurried into his office. "Zora's going to hire a man? What?" he joked, tossing a smile over his shoulder at Tate. "Did hell freeze over while I wasn't looking?" He rounded his desk and plopped down into his chair. Idly flipped through his messages, silently swore when he realized more than half of them were from *her*. His fingers involuntarily curled, crushing the notes in his hand.

Tate laughed, settled himself into the seat opposite him. "No. An opportune visit from Lady Luck and my superior poker skills are what brought about the phenomenon." His boss sighed, clearly wallowing in the victory of his coup.

"Dirty Poker, again, huh?" Ross replied, trying to force his irritated, preoccupied mind on their conversation. He conjured a brittle smile.

Zora and Tate's risqué card game was legendary among Tate's friends. By all accounts Zora was an abysmal poker player, yet that didn't keep the couple from continuing to play the game. Zora had once confided that even when she lost, she still won. As far as Ross was concerned, that one telling comment pretty much summed up their marriage.

In a time when more than half of all marriages ended in divorce—his parents' in-cluded—it was refreshing to see a couple who would undoubtedly go the distance. Not that their happily-ever-after engendered any latent desire to rush to the altar himself—not no, but hell no, Ross thought with an internal snort.

Maintaining a monogamous relationship was work and he already had a job, thank you very much. A job that he loved, where black was black and white was white and effort and loy-alty were rewarded accordingly. He avoided anything gray—emotions, feelings, guessing games, the unsure or the vague.

Furthermore, his parents' dysfunctional, mis-trustful, adulterous hate-fest had been a doozy, and after surviving that, he simply preferred to be single. If those weren't enough reasons to avoid emotional entanglements with the oppo-site sex, then his current situation most defi-nitely was.

He was being…harassed.

Actually, *stalked* worked better but it seemed so dramatic that Ross balked at the term. A lit-tle harassment he could handle—stalking im-plied he needed professional help.

Besides, at the moment—and pretty much every moment—he had more pressing matters to concern himself with than worrying about a possible significant other, lack thereof, or a thwarted lover who couldn't move on.

Like landing the Maxwell account.

The familiar burn of anticipation rushed through him, pushing the unpleasant thoughts aside. When word got out that Maxwell Commodities had been looking for a new firm, Tate had made sure that Hatcher Advertising was first in line for a shot at it. He'd then put his top executives on the job and Ross was fortunate enough to be counted among them.

But it wasn't good enough.

He wanted lead on this account.

And he was the logical choice because when it came to marketing men's products—no brag, just fact, he was the best in the firm. Maxwell Commodities marketed everything from men's toiletries to clothing as well as home fitness equipment and tools. The company catered exclusively to the male population and, while Ross admittedly didn't have any idea how to market women's products, he knew his stuff when it came to men. He was a guy, after all. His no-frills, no-bullshit style appealed to the man's man. Facts, statistics, specs. Those were the things men were interested in. Aesthetics, thank God, didn't enter the picture.

Landing lead on this account would garner national recognition, would put him in the inside lane on the fast track of his advertising career. Ross didn't think a man was measured by his success or any of that nonsense. He was simply competitive. Had always been that way. Hell, a guy couldn't play football—and every other sport imaginable—for more than a decade and come out any different. He wanted to be the best. When a knee injury in his senior year of high school had cost him a football career and a full-ride at LSU, Ross had been forced to direct his competitive efforts in another direction—college, then ultimately his career in advertising.

To that end, he *had* to land this account, because only the best could handle it.

"So who's the lucky guy?" Ross asked, tuning back into the conversation. "Anybody we know?"

Tate hesitated and a ghost of a smile hovered around his mouth. "As a matter of fact, yes. That's what I came to talk to you about."

"Me?" What did he have to do with it? Ross wondered, suppressing the growing urge to check his e-mail. He'd worked on a couple of new ideas for Maxwell last night and had forwarded them to his office account. Occasionally what seemed like creative genius in the wee hours of the morning turned out to be total shit after a few winks. He was curious to see what this morning's perspective brought.

"Yes, you." Tate paused, and for some reason that ominous silence rang like a death knell. "You see, it's not just *any* man that Zora has to hire—it's *you.*"

Ross stilled. Shock jimmied a disbelieving chuckle loose from his throat. *"What?"*

Tate smiled grimly. "It's you. You're the man she's hiring."

Stunned, Ross shook his head, waited for his frozen smile to thaw. "Er…no, she's not," he said flatly. Even if he were so inclined—which he most definitely was not—he didn't have the time. He had a damn job, one that he currently spent twelve-plus hours a day on. Furthermore, what in the hell would he do for Zora? What could he—a man—possibly do for a chick magazine?

Tate considered him for a moment, then sighed heavily. "I suppose I could call upon our years of friendship, ask you to do this for me simply because it would give me a small amount of petty satisfaction after listening to my wife repeatedly tell me that she'd never hire a man." Tate lifted his shoulders in a futile shrug. "But I can tell that it would be a waste of breath, so here's the deal. Do you want the Maxwell account?"

Ross blinked at the abrupt change in subject. "Of course I do."

"Then it's simple. If you agree to work for Zora, then it's yours. If not..." He winced lightly and let the implication hang in the silence.

Beyond stunned, Ross shook his head. Tate had a reputation for being a bit ruthless, but this was the first time he'd ever been on the receiving end of it. Arguing, Ross knew, would be pointless. Trying to make Tate change his mind once it was set was like bear-hunting with a BB gun. Utterly futile. He picked up a pen and tapped it on the desk. Resisted the urge to grind his teeth. "How long?"

"Only a week," Tate told him. He blew out an exasperated breath. "Look, I know I'm playing dirty on this one, but *I* won," he said desperately. With a somewhat manic gleam in his normally clear eyes, he leaned forward as though he were about to impart something very important. "Do you know what a rare occurrence that is with my wife? Do you have any idea?"

"You beat your wife at poker all the time, Tate," Ross returned flatly.

"Yeah, but this time it's different. I'm getting something that Zora's never had to give up—humility. Come on, Ross," he cajoled. "It's only a week. What's one week out of a lifetime? What's one measly week for the Maxwell account?"

Not much, he had to agree. Nevertheless, he didn't like being a part of Tate and Zora's poker games and he damned sure didn't like being blackmailed into getting an account that should have been his to start with.

Ross normally resisted all attempts to manage and maneuver him, but Tate, the intuitive bastard, had hit upon the one thing that he couldn't refuse—the Maxwell account. If he would have dangled anything else, Ross would have been able to say no.

But not this.

He wanted it. It was a trophy account—the one that would ultimately prove he'd arrived.

And, though he didn't appreciate Tate's method, he'd had the balls to lay it all on the line, so he had to respect him for that, if nothing else. Ross let go a breath and glared at him. "You're a sneaky bastard, Tate," he told him, letting him know that he wasn't completely off the hook.

"I know."

Resigned, Ross rubbed the bridge of his nose. "What exactly is it that I'm supposed to do?"

Seemingly relieved, Tate leaned back in his seat and winced. "That's the kicker. I don't know," he said grimly. "We're meeting Zora for lunch at Mama MoJo's at noon."

Ross shot him a hard look. "But it's only a week, right?"

Tate nodded. "Right."

"Fine," Ross told him wearily. Hell, he could stand anything for a week, especially if it meant the Maxwell account would be his.

2

THREE HOURS LATER Ross's steps slowed as he entered the eclectic café and the grim realization that he'd been wrong—that there was *one thing* that he couldn't take for a week—hit him because that very *thing* was sitting at their table with Zora—*Frankie Salvaterra.*

"You didn't tell me Mouth would be here," Ross said tightly. Equal parts anticipation, dread and desire coalesced in his gut, pushed his pulse rate up to pre-stroke level. His skin prickled, his stomach parachuted and his loins ignited into an inferno of repressed lust.

Regrettably, Frankie always had that effect on him.

"That's because I didn't know," Tate returned from the side of his mouth as he made his way across the room. He, too, suddenly looked a little uneasy, a fact Ross didn't find the least bit reassuring.

Having spotted them, Zora smiled and waved them over. Frankie turned then, and that dark-as-sin gaze tangled with his. Her ripe mouth curled into a woefully familiar mockery of a grin, the barest hint of a smile, and that one pro-voking gesture somehow managed to be simul-taneously superior and sexy.

And, as usual, it annoyed the hell out of him. He swallowed a long-suffering sigh.

Furthermore, to make matters worse—and truthfully, he wouldn't have thought that would have been possible—Frankie had looked en-tirely too happy to suit his taste…because if Frankie was happy it could only be because she knew that he would soon be supremely *un*happy. Clearly Zora had filled her in on the present sit-uation and Ms. Merciless had tagged along to silently chortle over his misfortune.

"You have no idea what she wants me to do?" Ross asked again. His gaze drifted to Frankie once more and he watched as she and Zora shared a conspiratorial smile. Oh, hell, Ross thought as dread formed a tight ball in his belly. This didn't bode well. Not well at all. His insides clenched and he stifled a groan.

"None," Tate replied as they neared the table. He bent and brushed a kiss over his wife's cheek and murmured a warm greeting.

"Zora, Frankie," Ross said, giving them each a glance in turn, before taking his seat. Though he'd only spared half a second, had barely glanced at her at all, that one meager look had been all Ross needed to catalogue every pertinent detail when it came to Frankie.

Simply put, she was a classic Italian beauty. Long black hair, cut in lengthy layers that framed an elegant yet striking face. Large almond-shaped dark eyes, sleek dramatic brows, creamy olive skin and a mouth that inspired more than a few erotic dreams. Her lips were full, lush and unbelievably provocative. She was petite but very generously curved and she moved with a careless sort of grace that was, quite frankly, fascinating—*mesmerizing*—to watch.

Ross inwardly snorted. God knows, there had been times when dragging his eyes off of her had been almost impossible. Were that not enough, for reasons which escaped him, the Almighty had further blessed her with a keen mind and a diabolically sharp wit. Ross had found himself verbally flayed many times by that Ginsu tongue of hers and he grimly suspected that it was about to happen again.

It was a cruel joke really, Ross thought, mentally bracing himself, to package such a mind and body with the personality of a waspish hellcat. Crueler still that he actually *looked forward* to tangling with her, that he wanted her so desperately that it almost frightened him. Thankfully, fear was an emotion he refused to acknowledge, otherwise he'd undoubtedly be in trouble.

A beat later he felt her gaze slide over him, caught the vaguest curve of a smile, and the unease that had settled like a stone in his gut grew increasingly heavier. Annoyed, he looked away. A single hot oath sizzled on his tongue, but miraculously, he held it.

"I think I'm going to have the grilled chicken salad," Zora said, casually perusing the menu. "What about you, honey? Have you decided what you want?"

Tate nodded, set his menu aside and absently scratched his chest. "Yeah. I'm in the mood for jambalaya."

Ross resisted the pressing urge to roll his eyes. He was in the mood to get this over with, to cease and desist with the idle chitchat when they all knew they were here to plunge him into some unknown hell.

"That sounds good," Frankie chimed in. "I think I'll have that as well. Know what you want, Ross?" she asked with a touch of humor.

To leave, and from the knowing twinkle in her eye she'd evidently figured it out. "Er...the usual, I think. A MoJo burger and an order of fries."

A waitress came, took their order, then soon returned and delivered drinks. Once she left, Ross decided that it was time to put an end to the meaningless chatter and cut to the chase.

He manufactured a smile that fell several degrees shy of pleasant and aimed it at Zora. "Tate has blackmailed me into coming to work for you at *CHiC* for the next week. Wanna fill me in on exactly what I'll be doing?"

Zora looked up, smoothly set her drink aside.

She seemed to have been waiting for him to broach the subject. "Sure. You'll be working with Frankie." She nodded toward her friend. "That's why she's here."

If working for *CHiC* had been the directive that sent him to hell, then working *with* Frankie was the equivalent of being ushered to the very gates of Hades. For whatever reason—premonition, bad luck, bad karma—he had the grimmest feeling that the rest of what Zora had to tell him would send him over the threshold straight to the deepest nether regions of the underworld.

Zora smiled, serenely enjoying his discomfort. "As you know, Frankie is *CHiC's* Carnal Contessa. Our *sex*pert, if you will."

He was fully aware of her job, what it entailed, and had read each and every column. One had to know one's enemy, after all, and Ross had perceived many interesting facets of her personality through her advice, seeds of insight she'd unwittingly sown. Furthermore, there was something incredibly attractive about a woman who could speak freely about sex, the ultimate taboo. Frankie clearly reveled in her sexuality, clearly enjoyed every nuance of male/female ritual.

What he failed to see was how he could possibly work with her.

"As you know, *CHiC* has just launched the new glossy format. Over the next week Frankie will be touring the country to promote the new look. A five-city tour, to be precise." She calmly sipped her drink and delivered the coup de grace. "You will accompany her."

Ross blinked. It took a minute to believe his ears, but only a nanosecond to absorb the implication—and he didn't like it. A five-city tour? Accompany her? But that meant he'd be gone, unable to work, unable to polish the pitch for the Maxwell account. Hell, he hadn't had the time to play around with *CHiC* for a week to begin with, but at least he would have had his evenings to himself. He could have worked from home. This— Ross shook his head and felt his expression blacken. *This would not do.*

His gaze flew to Tate, who wore a somewhat slack-jawed smirk. "I can't be gone for a week," he said, his voice throbbing with the effort not to shout. "I can't just leave at the drop of a hat. What about work? What about the Maxwell account?" Ross blew out a harsh breath. "This is ridiculous. I can't do it." His gaze drifted to Zora. "I'm sorry, but you'll have to find something else for me to do."

Zora shook her head, offered a smile that distinctly lacked sympathy. "I'm afraid that's out of the question. This is what I need you to do." She looked at her husband. "I thought you said he'd agreed?"

"He'd agreed to work for *CHiC*," Tate responded tightly. "However, when I asked him—"

Ross snorted. "Blackmailed, buddy. You didn't *ask*," he interjected.

Tate shot him a glare. "—I had no idea that you'd need him to be away from home for the next week. This sheds a completely different light on things, Zora," he told her, clearly irritated.

Zora grinned happily. Though she didn't move, Ross got the impression she wanted to bounce in her seat. "You're right. It means that you forfeit and I win."

A muscle worked in Tate's jaw and a martial light suddenly glinted in his tense gaze, one Ross instinctively knew didn't bode well for his cause. "I'll put Brad on everything but the Maxwell account in your absence, Ross. You can still work on it from the road. We'll arrange a mobile office and I'll make sure a dedicated team is in place to see to anything you might need on this end."

Ross dragged in a harsh breath. "Tate—"

Tate continued to glare at his wife. "I will not forfeit. She's not going to win. Take it or leave it. Those are the terms."

"You should probably tell him the rest so that he can make an informed decision, right, Zora?" Frankie leaned back in her chair, crossed her arms over her chest and regarded him with something close to pitying amusement.

His gaze bounced from Frankie to Zora and he felt his eyes widen in shocked disbelief. *The rest?* There was *more?* As it stood, he'd have to be on the road with Frankie—hell, in and of itself—and yet there was more?

Ross smirked, looked heavenward for patience, for divine intervention before he did something stupid. Like telling his boss and his evil wife to shove it. "Do tell, Zora," he said sardonically. "I do want to make an 'informed decision.'"

"Very well," Zora replied. "You'll be accompanying Frankie as *CHiC*'s Duke of Desire. You, too, will dole out sex advice, speak for the male population."

Ross blinked, certain he couldn't possibly have heard her correctly. "Come again?"

A familiar feminine chuckle sounded. Frankie's, no doubt, the vindictive witch. He could think of a million other ways to put that carnal mouth to better use, Ross thought, as his blood began to boil.

"You'll go as the Duke of Desire," Zora repeated. Her lips quivered with the urge to smile and an evil twinkle danced in her triumphant gaze. She slid her husband a glance, then met his gaze once more. "You'll do exactly what Frankie does, only you'll speak for the male audience."

It was that triumphant gaze, that laughter at his expense that checked Ross's immediate impulse to tell them all to go to hell. And it was a strong impulse, almost overwhelming.

But that look simply wasn't acceptable.

It strummed his *let's-rumble* nerve, hit his competitive vein releasing a flood of you'll-wish-you-were-never-born cutthroat blood that instantly pushed a lazy do-or-die grin up his lips. They wanted to play, did they? Fine. He was up for it.

He passed a hand over his face. "Let me get this straight. You want me to go with Frankie and talk about sex for the next week?" he asked. He let his gaze drift to her, then purposely over her, and had the pleasure of watching that annoying smile she'd been wearing slowly capsize.

Zora nodded, sensing his abrupt change in mood as well. She stilled. "That sums it up nicely, yes."

He looked at Tate. "And the Maxwell account is mine when I get back?"

"That's right."

Ross grinned, and despite the fact he was wound tighter than an eight-day clock, he lifted one shoulder in a negligent shrug. "Then it's a no-brainer. Count me in."

"Excellent," Zora replied. She stood and nudged her husband, who belatedly left his chair. "We'll get ours to go. Frankie, you take a long lunch, fill Ross in on the particulars and I'll see you back at the office." She and Tate hurried off before Frankie could voice the protest that had formed silently on her lips.

"Looks like it's just me and you," he told her, enjoying his advantage. "Guess we'd better get used to it. A whole week," he needled significantly. *"Together."*

Frankie's gorgeous face went comically blank. Obviously she'd been so caught up in his future misery that she'd failed to consider her own.

Ross's mood instantly improved—perhaps he should enlighten her.

THINGS HAD GONE EXACTLY as she'd imagined right up until five minutes ago, Frankie thought as her former glee turned into furious despair. Ross had reacted much as she'd predicted for the initial part of the lunch, then he'd surprised her by capitulating so easily. She hadn't expected his abrupt change of heart and, quite honestly, the fact that he was taking this so well infuriated the living hell out of her.

He wasn't supposed to take it well.

He was supposed to stomp and roar like an outraged elephant. He was not supposed to dismiss the next week as the Duke of Desire as mildly amusing, then dig into his lunch as though he didn't have a care in the world.

It was exceedingly unsporting of him.

"Look, Ross," Frankie said, coating her patronizing tone with a hard layer of ice. "I don't think it's going to be as easy as you think."

"What?" he asked. He grinned that lazy, sexy grin, the one that never failed to simultaneously turn her on and irritate the hell out of her. "I'm going to give sex advice. How hard can it be?" He winked at her. "I happen to be an expert."

Frankie snorted, staunchly ignored the flash-fire that quickly spread over her thighs. "That's a matter of opinion and, just for clarification, not yours." God, could a man be any more conceited?

"It's a fact, and can be authenticated if you require proof."

To her horror, she felt a blush creep up her neck. She swallowed and donned an exasperated expression. "Trust me, that won't be necessary. My point is, you'll be representing the magazine. You'll need to be careful what sort of advice you dole out, otherwise you'll make *CHiC* look bad. Which for obvious reasons isn't the goal." She snapped her napkin into her lap. "In short, you won't be able to act like your typical obnoxious know-it-all self."

Looking irritatingly unconcerned, Ross chuckled low and sprawled back into his seat. "Now that's the pot calling the kettle black if I've ever heard one."

Annoyed, Frankie picked up her spoon and chased a piece of sausage around the bowl. "Furthermore," she added, "merely having sex does not make you an expert."

Ross cast her a twinkling glance, washed a bite of his burger down with a deep drink of his iced tea. "Yeah…but having sex *a lot* does."

Frankie's fingers tightened around her utensil and she futilely wondered if it were possible to claw out her mind's eye. "That's more than I needed to know." Way more. Hell, she knew he was experienced—from what she'd covertly gleaned from Zora, Ross was never without a date, had to practically beat the women off his sexy hide with a stick. Furthermore, she also instinctively knew he was the expert he claimed to be, but the reminder played havoc with her senses and she'd just as soon not hear it.

"Really?" he said, evidently enjoying this suggestive line of conversation. A droll smile rolled around his lips, and those sexy-as-hell kaleidoscope eyes crinkled at the corners. "I would have thought that I'd need to list my experience. That you might even need to call a few references for this job." His voice dropped to a sensual purr. "Or, maybe you could *interview* me personally," he suggested. "Check my job performance, make sure that I'm competent enough to be your Duke of Desire."

The innuendo in that low, hazy voice conjured an image of her *interviewing* him until her eyes rolled back in her head. *Cool sheets, hot naked bodies, candlelight and massage oil. Hot, hard and fast, then slow, easy and deliberate.* Her feminine muscles clenched, forcing a shuddering breath from her lungs. "No," she said tightly, blinking the vision from her mind. "That won't be necessary. Dammit, Ross, you're not taking this seriously."

"Why should I?" he countered, seemingly oblivious to the fact that she'd just produced her own mental porn film, featuring them in the starring roles. "We both know I've been manipulated into this. I became a pawn in Zora and Tate's poker game—and you're deluding yourself if you think you aren't as well."

Frankie rolled her eyes. "You're full of it, you know it, Ross?"

He laughed and gave her an odd expression, one that left her with the unhappy sensation that he was privy to something she was not. "Now this is new," he said consideringly. "You're usually a lot quicker on the uptake than this."

Frankie scowled at him. "What the hell are you talking about?"

"Zora lost the bet," he said with exaggerated patience, "and yet she's obviously very happy with the way things have turned out. If she lost, just what exactly had it been that she stood to win?"

Frankie paused. She hadn't thought of it that way. "I don't know," Frankie said slowly. And it was an excellent question. In fact, it irritated her that he'd thought of it first.

Ross took up another fry and pointed it at her before popping it into his mouth. "I don't know for sure, but you can bet your sweet little Italian ass that it had something to do with me *and* with you, otherwise, we wouldn't be sitting here, and we damned sure wouldn't be spending the next week together." Ross snorted. "Duke of Desire, my ass. That was simply icing on somebody's cake and if I had to hazard a guess, I'd say it was on *your* boss's, not *mine*."

Ross stood and tossed a few bills on the table. "If I'm going to be gone for the next week, I've got to get organized. Find someone to dog-sit, swing by my house every few days to collect the mail, and all that jazz. Come by my place tonight and we can go over whatever else I need to know then."

"But—"

He leaned forward and lowered his voice. The combined proximity of that sexy gaze, that intimate rasp and his particular woodsy fragrance made her body sing like a tuning fork, her brain melt, ready to believe anything. "And just so you know, Ms. *Sex*pert, I'll be one helluva Duke of Desire because I've forgotten more about sex than you'll ever know…unless I develop a death wish and decide to teach you."

Frankie blinked drunkenly for several seconds and by the time her sluggish brain had manufactured a comeback, Ross had already made it to the door. "Develop a death wish," she muttered under her breath, silently cursing her roaring pulse. Her eyes narrowed and a low growl vibrated the back of her throat.

As though sleeping with her wouldn't be the best thing to ever happen to him. Someone needed to teach *him* a lesson, Frankie thought. A good moral one like *"pride goeth before the fall."*

Death wish, her ass. She smiled grimly. By the end of next week, he'd undoubtedly be wishing that he was dead.

3

AFTER COMING HOME to a bouquet of flowers on his front porch, two lengthy I-miss-you, this-can't-be-over letters in his mail box and half a dozen hang-up calls on his answering machine, the idea of leaving town for a week—even with thorn-in-his-side Frankie—had gained considerable appeal.

Honestly, Ross thought with a disgusted grunt as he tossed the letters aside and systematically erased each of the messages, how much longer could this go on? He'd dodged calls from Amy—the ex who didn't get the "ex" part—all morning and afternoon, and knew that the only reason she hadn't "dropped by"—an irritatingly frequent occurrence—was because she was working. She'd shared that little tidbit in one of her many messages.

Ross had been dating since his early teens, knew the ins and outs of proper dating and break-up etiquette. He wasn't a cheap date, did his best to be respectful and attentive and never tried to push things to an intimate level unless he was completely sure of two things—mutual consent and the understanding that sex wasn't a precursor to a lasting relationship.

The moment he felt a woman change the rules, sensed that they were trying to move things beyond a purely recreational level, he very politely, very carefully bailed.

Dates one and two with Amy had been great. Date three she'd spent the night. Date four she'd asked for a key. He hadn't given her one, of course, but that hadn't stopped her from "surprising" him with dinner—at his house—on date five.

He'd come home to find his living room rearranged, a casserole in the oven, and her toothbrush, toiletries and a good portion of her wardrobe in his closet.

The minor note of alarm he'd heard when she asked for the key had been nothing compared to the deafening sound of mental warning he'd experienced then.

Rather than break things off by natural degrees, Ross had—as diplomatically as he could under the circumstances—ended their relationship. He'd speedily loaded her chicken pot pie, pantyhose and other belongings into her car and sent her on her way.

Then he'd changed the locks.

There'd been something…off about the entire exchange which had made him a little nervous.

For good reason, it now seemed. Though he'd repeatedly made his feelings plain—*"This isn't working for me, we're finished, it's over."*—short of shouting *"Leave me alone, you psycho freak!"*, Ross didn't know what else to do.

He'd always considered freezing a woman out by avoiding phone calls the cowardly, disrespectful approach, but during the past week he'd had to resort to that tactic. Being tactful but honest—then *brutally* honest—hadn't worked. Ross had figured that if he simply quit responding, she'd eventually give up and move on.

Not so.

If anything, she seemed to have redoubled her efforts to make him change his mind. Seemed more determined than ever to win him back. It was annoying, not to mention…creepy. In his opinion—or any right-thinking person's opinion for that matter—they hadn't known each other long enough for her to have developed such an attachment.

At any rate, he didn't have the time to linger over the issue any longer. He had too much to do.

Like getting ready for this pointless week-long jaunt around the country with Frankie.

Her beautiful smug face instantly surfaced in his weary mind, causing a simultaneous rush of irritation and longing. An odd mix, for sure, but one that he'd grown accustomed to since their mutual friends tied the knot. He'd met Frankie—as well as the rest of Zora's *CHiC* posse—at a cook-out shortly after Zora and Tate had taken their relationship public. That had been something, Ross remembered. When Tate—the man who'd written *What Women Really Want—Reading between the Sighs,* who the *Times* had dubbed "The Last True Bachelor" and Zora, the founding president of *Chicks-In-Charge,* the poster child for Girl Power—had paired up, the press had had a field day with it.

An ordinary couple probably wouldn't have been able to withstand the scrutiny, but Tate and Zora had been so committed to each other—so in love—that they'd pulled through without a hitch.

Though birthdays eluded him and he'd never managed to commit his social security number to memory, Ross could remember the exact moment he'd seen Frankie, the precise instant he'd felt her presence. He'd been keeping Tate company at the grill, had just lifted a bottle to his lips when he'd caught sight of her out of the corner of his eye. The strangest feeling had come over him, one that to this day he still couldn't name, didn't even attempt to try.

He'd stilled. Sound had receded, every sense had gone on point, the bottom dropped out of his stomach, and for all intents and purposes, he might as well have been a stallion catching the scent of a mare.

It wasn't just that she was gorgeous—though, he thought with a broken laugh, God knows there was no denying that—or the fact that she was sexy as hell. Frankie had possessed some other indefinable something that made *her,* in particular, utterly fascinating to him. There was a gut-level, knee-jerk attraction he'd never experienced before and instinctively knew he'd never feel again.

Regrettably, five seconds beyond their introduction—the one he'd taken great pains to *casually* force—for reasons he'd never understood, she'd taken an instant dislike to him, given him one of those provoking superior looks, opened her mouth, and that keen fascination had become hopelessly tangled with equal parts of annoyance, irritation and, gallingly, lust.

Since then the attraction had worsened right along with their ability to get along. She never missed an opportunity to zing him—went out of her way, as a matter of fact—and rather than ignoring her or giving her the cold shoulder—the mature, not to mention sane approach—he'd upped the ante until they'd turned clever bickering into an Olympic sport.

He'd rather have Olympic sex with her, but knew he had a better chance of being plucked out of his office to play quarterback for the Dallas Cowboys than maneuvering her delectable bod into bed. Was she attracted to him? Yes. Hell, he had enough experience with the opposite sex to deduce when one wanted him. Like him, Ross imagined that Frankie purposely overcompensated with sarcasm to mask the attraction.

But unlike him, she'd never act on it—she was too damn stubborn, a fact he'd noted quite forcibly when they'd tangled over hosting the wedding reception.

He'd jokingly—*jokingly,* geez didn't she have a sense of humor?—suggested Hooters and she'd exploded like a hot cola can, spewing her disgust and anger at him. Citing his lamentable lack of taste, she'd promptly taken over and only by sheer force of will was he able to inject a little of his own ideas into the final arrangements.

The minute he'd gotten back to the office after that shanghai lunch, Ross had gone directly to Tate's office and hounded him until he'd called Zora and gathered further details about the upcoming trip. He'd just as soon not be dependent on Frankie for all the facts, thank you very much and, since his landing the Maxwell account depended on him pulling off this week-long stint, he thought it prudent to make sure that he was aware of everything they would be doing.

He'd gotten the schedule and, though some of the flights and appearances were a little tight, there was still a window of time between each city that would allow him to work on the Maxwell account. He had to keep that in mind, Ross told himself. Undoubtedly the only thing that would keep him sane on this trip was the opportunity to immerse himself in work. He felt a smile tug at the corner of his mouth.

Immersing himself in Frankie was certainly out of the question.

As though the mere thought of her had conjured her out of thin air, Ross heard a knock at his front door. His neck tightened with tension and he let go a short breath.

Belatedly wishing he'd taken a moment to straighten up, he made his way to the foyer and braced himself for the climate shock—the combination of her chilly disposition and the blazing heat of attraction never failed to make him feel like he'd come down with a virulent case of the flu.

Frankie-itis, he thought with a faint smile.

He was about to be infected again and, re-grettably, modern medicine would never be able to cure what ailed him. He grimly suspected mouth-to-mouth—her mouth to his—and the hot, frantic exchange of bodily fluids would provide a temporary antidote…and he'd un-doubtedly require frequent vaccinations.

ROSS'S HOUSE was not what she expected.

On the too many occasions Frankie had thought about Ross kicking back in his house-of-sex lair, she'd imagined a traditional brick rancher with a small, spare lawn. Something low-maintenance that allowed him to pursue his bachelor activities without being hindered by mundane domestic chores.

Feeling unaccountably wary at the idea that Ross didn't fit into the shallow little niche she'd put him in, Frankie stowed her sunglasses, stared at the house and tried to drum up the nerve to get out of her car.

The white double-galleried house with its sweeping porches, gabled roof and asymmetri-cal design hardly fit the confines of her uncharitable imaginings. Live oaks dripping with Spanish moss shaded the perfectly maintained grounds, and after she'd managed to wrap her mind around the fact that *Ross Hartford* lived *here,* she could discern certain touches in which his admittedly compelling personality expressed itself.

There were distinctly masculine lines to the outdoor furniture and he'd planted hearty shrubs—boxwoods, dwarf Chinese Holly, and yew—as well as miniature roses and wisteria. This wasn't just a *house,* Frankie realized as a peculiar sensation winged through her chest, it was a *home,* and a lovely one at that. She inwardly snorted. It was a far cry from her little shotgun house on the other side of town, that was for sure. Not that she didn't love her house. She did. It was small, cozy and charming. But most importantly, it was *hers*. Her sanctuary. Her retreat. She needed that kind of—

The sound of a car door slamming behind her snapped her out of her reverie. Frankie's gaze shot to the rearview mirror and she discovered a florist delivery vehicle had pulled in behind her. She watched the delivery man disappear to the rear of the van and felt her brow wrinkle into a curious frown. What? she wondered. Had he ordered some fresh flowers?

She patiently waited behind the wheel until the delivery guy re-emerged from behind the van. One look at the arrangement he carried made her fingers tighten on the steering wheel as an emotion mortifyingly like jealousy bolted through her, forcing a disgusted breath from her lungs.

Lip-shaped Mylar balloons which had cute little sayings on them like *Sexy, Hot Stuff, Sizzle* and *Cutie* were attached to a stuffed bear wearing red silky boxers. Evidently he was so good in bed women felt compelled to send him gifts which blatantly rhapsodized his sexual abilities and had the unfortunate side effect of further catering to his massive ego.

But not if she had anything to say about it.

Frankie vaulted out of her car and smoothly intercepted the delivery guy. "Let me take these for you," she offered sweetly. "I'm going right in."

"Thanks," he replied, looking somewhat harried. "This is the third time I've been by here today."

Frankie fumbled the bear. "The third time?" she repeated, her eyes widening. She figured Ross kept a ready cache of female friends, but this?

"Yeah. Gets stuff all the time, this guy," he said with a shake of his head. He waggled his brows. "I'd sure like to know his secret." And with that parting comment, he made the return trek to his vehicle.

Frankie resisted the urge to grind her teeth. She told herself that the sick feeling in her belly wasn't jealousy and labeled it disgust. It was utterly pathetic, she decided, when Ross Hartford got more flowers and gifts than she did.

She batted a balloon from in front of her face and made the grim walk to the front door, then knocked and waited. She heard the lock tumble back, giving her enough time to push her lips into a patently false smile.

"Ah, darling," he said with mock humility, spying the gift. "You didn't have to bring me anything."

Frankie shoved the balloon bouquet at him. "*I* didn't. I merely helped an overworked delivery man. According to him, a few more trips to your house and he'll be able to retire."

His smile slipped a fraction and a fleeting frown raced across his face, but he recovered so quickly she wondered if she'd imagined it. "Very cute," he said, taking the bear from her. He stepped back so that she could walk past. "I see I'll have your particular brand of humor to look forward to on our trip."

Frankie sailed past him and coolly glanced around the foyer. Good taste, too, she thought, unreasonably annoyed. "And I'll have your ego to contend with, so by my estimation that makes us even." Hardwood floors, nice moldings, quality furniture, she noted with envy. Surprisingly, their tastes were very similar.

She turned and caught the wretch scowling at the card attached to the bouquet. "What?" she asked with a pointed smirk. "Would you have preferred roses?"

Seemingly distracted, Ross looked up. "No," he said slowly. "I would have preferred nothing at all."

Frankie feigned fierce concentration and pretended to take a note. "Conceited *and* ungrateful."

Ross set the bouquet on an antique bureau

next to the front door and heaved a long-suffering sigh, one to her frustration she found oddly endearing. "And so it begins," he said, passing a hand over his face. "I need a beer. Want one?"

Frankie nodded. "Sure." She followed him down the hall, through a spacious parlor with comfortable furniture, quality artwork and the odd antique, then finally into the kitchen. Glass-fronted cabinets, stainless-steel gourmet appliances and granite countertops seamlessly melded the old with the new and it was immediately obvious given the window herb garden and top-of-the-line cookware that Ross knew his way around a kitchen. Though she didn't want to admit it, there was something intensely sexy about that. About a guy who could cook in the kitchen as well as the bedroom.

As if she needed to notice anything else sexy about him, she thought with an inward snort of despair. Frankie watched him smoothly pull open the fridge and snag a couple of beers.

He'd changed out of his corporate uniform and had donned a pair of low-slung olive cargo shorts and a white button-up short-sleeved shirt that he'd neglected to fully fasten. Several buttons were loose from their closures and the intriguing patch of golden masculine hair and tanned muscle peeking through was enough to give her small heart palpitations. He wore a leather cord around his neck with a small silver pendent she recognized as the Chinese symbol for strength. She ought to recognize it—she had the same symbol tattooed just above her left ankle. His feet were bare and his hair was mussed, giving him a slightly bohemian look. Effortlessly sexy, Frankie thought as another flame of heat flared in her belly.

Ross opened a beer and handed it to her. She'd barely muttered a thanks when a curious sound reached her ears. A galloping, clicking sort of noise that seemed to be swiftly approaching the kitchen. She frowned, shot Ross a look. "What the hell is—"

The ugliest dog she'd ever seen bounded into the kitchen, sliding across the hardwood floor in answer to her question. It ran straight at her, then planted its short, stumpy legs on her shins and howled up at her in the most pitiful-sounding wail she'd ever heard.

"Dammit, Otis," Ross muttered with gruff affection, a lopsided grin tilting his lips. "Get off her. She's not sharing."

"Not sharing what?" Frankie asked, perplexed, as the dog let out another unearthly howl. He gazed longingly at her, his great brown eyes pleading. For what exactly she couldn't discern.

Ross wearily set his unopened drink aside and pulled another bottle out of the refrigerator. "Your beer," he said matter-of-factly. "He heard me pop the top. He's got a drinking problem."

Frankie gaped at him. *"What?"*

"He's an alcoholic." Ross popped the top off the new bottle and calmly squatted down and poured it into Otis's bowl, as though sharing a beer with a dog were a completely normal thing. The instant he'd heard the second bottle open, Otis had dropped his front paws back onto the floor and raced to his bowl, then greedily— loudly—lapped up his fix. He patted the dog on the back. "There you go, buddy. Drink up."

Appalled, Frankie didn't know which issue to address first. The fact that Ross had managed to turn his pet into an alcoholic or that he was continuing to feed his habit. It was unconscionable.

How could he do something so cruel, so patently wrong to an animal she could tell he obviously had a small measure of feeling for. She scowled. Undoubtedly Otis-the-beer-drinking-dog was a source of entertainment for Ross and his bored, twisted friends.

After giving the dog one more pat, he stood up and looked at her. "Ah," he sighed as his lips quirked with droll humor. "I can tell by the mulish set of your lovely jaw that you've leapt to some unflattering, incorrect assumptions. So before you start slinging allegations and insults why don't you let me give you a few facts."

"Be my guest," she said tightly.

Ross slouched back against the counter. "*I* didn't turn Otis into an alcoholic—his former owner did. He'd belonged to an old bum who hung out on the waterfront. When he died, Otis wound up at the animal shelter, which is where I found him. And contrary to what you think you just saw, I did not give my dog beer," he said, his voice laced with a hint of patient exasperation. "Hell, I'm not an idiot. That was *near* beer." He pulled a shrug. "He likes the malt flavor and according to my vet, it's completely harmless." He quirked a pointed brow. "Does that answer all your questions?"

Frankie nodded, reluctantly impressed with the idea that Ross possessed enough compassion to choose a wounded pet who would require more time and attention. That took loyalty, a dying commodity these days. She swallowed, once again forced to move him out of another preconceived niche, and belatedly wondered how many other times she might be forced to do that over the coming week.

None, she hoped. The very idea gave her pause.

The only way she'd managed her attraction to Ross thus far was by finding things to dislike about him. In fact, she'd taken one look at him and felt things she'd never felt for another living soul. His sex appeal had blasted into her like a wave of heat from a stoked boiler, literally stopping her in her tracks. Her mouth had lost every bit of its moisture and a funky sense of familiarity had settled in her gut, as though some part of her recognized him despite the fact that they'd never met. She'd fallen into those kaleidoscope eyes and what she'd seen there had sent her into a panic the likes of which she'd never experienced before.

But what she'd *felt* had scared the living hell out of her.

Undoubtedly if she let herself so much as like him, she'd turn into one of his many pathetic groupies, sending him moronic balloon bouquets and begging for his time like a mutt at the back door of a meat market.

Not no, but hell no.

She *would not* be her mother. Even if she thought men were trustworthy—which she didn't—she would not give so much of herself to another person that she wouldn't have any respect left for herself. And, though she hated it— and no small part of the reason why she strived to hate him—she instinctively knew, had known since the first instant she'd seen *him*—that Ross Hartford was *the one guy* who could make her do that…if she let him.

Frankie let go an unsteady breath and made a valiant effort to tune back into the conversation. "As a matter of fact, I do have one question," she said in answer to the one he'd asked her.

Ross wore an it-figured look, that barest hint

of a smile that never failed to make her toes curl in her shoes. "Oh? What's that?"

"Why Otis?"

The corner of his mouth tucked into a grin. "Isn't it obvious?"

"If it was I wouldn't be asking."

"I'm a big Andy Griffith fan. If you'll remember, Otis was—"

"—the town drunk," Frankie finished knowingly as the tidbit clicked into place. The name drew a reluctant smile, then a chuckle.

He pulled another negligent shrug, cast a fond look at the dog. "It seemed to fit."

Frankie watched the dog continue to greedily lap at the bowl and had to agree. She let go a small sigh. "I guess so."

"So," he said, casting her another glance. "Why don't we head back to the living room and you can fill me in on our itinerary for the next week."

Frankie nodded. The sooner she got this over with the better. Being here with Ross—in his element, in particular—was wreaking havoc on her senses. It humanized him in a way that was wholly unexpected. She could only imagine what state her nerves—not to mention her libido—would be in after seven unrelenting days spent in his company.

Her gaze dropped to his ass as she followed him out of the kitchen and she resisted the pressing urge to whimper.

God help me, she thought. She was surely going to need it.

4

"I'VE WRITTEN everything down for you, Charley, but if you have any questions, or have any problems, then you've got my schedule and you've got my cell." Ross loaded the last of his bags into the cargo area, then shut the hatch. "Remember what I said about visitors. With the exception of your mother, *no one* is allowed in."

A necessary precaution in light of Amy's disturbing habit of showing up. Though he knew it sounded paranoid, he could easily see her shunting Charley out the door and once again ensconcing herself at his house. Another thought struck on the heels of that grim scenario. "And don't tell anyone where I'm at. The people that matter already know where I'm going. I'll be checking in, making sure Otis is okay."

Charley Rikard shoved his glasses back up

his nose. "Don't worry. I'll take good care of him."

Ross didn't have a single doubt. Charley was Ross's neighbor, a responsible college brainiac who still lived at home and whose idea of a good time was playing Internet chess and various computer games. Ross wouldn't have to worry about coming home to a frat party or having his house trashed. Wouldn't have to worry about anything, as a matter of fact, and as an added bonus, Charley would be out from under his mother's thumb for a little while.

Mrs. Rikard had lost her husband during Charley's freshman year of high school and, having been lectured on the perils of raising a teenage boy alone, overcompensated by wrapping the apron strings around the child's neck. She'd raised a good kid, no doubt, but had socially stunted him in the process.

As far as Ross knew he'd never had a friend over, much less been on a date. Ross did little things—having him house sit, taking him to ball games and the occasional movie—to try and haul him out of his nerd shell. It had gradually begun to work. His next project was to get the kid laid. He cast Charley a glance and inwardly grimaced. But first he'd have to take him shopping and show him a little something about current fashion trends. The Bugs Bunny T-shirt and hi-topped sneakers would have to go.

He clapped the young man on the shoulder. "All right, then. I'm gonna head out." He mentally ran down the list of things he needed to take and nodded to himself when he decided he had everything. Or at least everything of importance. Namely his laptop, printer and fax, and all of his notes regarding the Maxwell account. If he'd forgotten toiletries, he could buy them. Confident that he was ready, Ross slid behind the wheel.

"Have a good trip," Charley called as he backed out of the drive.

Ross managed a thin smile and waved in return. Having a "good" trip was stretching it, but hopefully he could have a passable one. Frankie had been surprisingly organized and honest when sharing their itinerary night before last. He suspected she'd been organized so that she could make their meeting as short as possible. Other than roasting him over the trophy wall in his living room—"Are you compensating for something?" she'd needled mercilessly—she hadn't been inclined to stay and socialize.

Ross knew that Frankie had looked at all of those trophies and assumed that he was holding onto his misspent youth, the athlete he used to be.

She thought wrong.

Losing the opportunity to play at a college level had been a blow, yes, but watching his parents' marriage dissolve along with his football career had been much worse. For years his athletic ability had held them together. As a boy he'd signed up to play *everything*, had made it a point to excel at *everything*. So long as they could talk about how well he'd played, or rehash a game, they weren't fighting, drinking, or running around on each other. Those trophies—MVP, All-Star, All-State—were more than just testaments to his physical talents, they represented a happier time, one he'd worked extremely hard for.

Besides, Ross thought with a bitter smile, his mother and father had fought over them during the divorce and considering *he'd* been the one to earn them—and considering they were *his*—Ross thought it best that they stay with him.

Of course he hadn't told her any of this, though to his complete astonishment he'd actually been tempted. His desire for her to know the truth—for her to know that he wasn't some vain washed-up has-been who couldn't get over his high school dreams—had almost trumped his need for privacy. Luckily, she'd gathered her purse and stood as he was readying his mouth to spill his guts, preventing him from making a huge fool of himself.

Hell, he didn't know why he cared what she thought. Furthermore, arming her of all people—she, who delighted in mocking him at every turn—with personal secrets was the height of stupidity.

Just like occasionally driving by her house was.

Ross had made a grand show of taking down her address last night, but in truth he'd known exactly where she lived. He'd snagged her address from the phone book after that ill-fated cook-out, then, for no other reason than to see where she lived—a completely ridiculous excuse—he'd gotten the directions using one of the online mapping sites.

It was odd the things one could learn while

doing the occasional drive-by. Frankie, he knew, liked pansies and mums—particularly the purple varieties—and she liked her space. Guarded her privacy, her nest, he thought with a fond smile. She never had company and her blinds were always closed.

He cruised from his house to hers on autopilot and found himself somewhat surprised as he turned the car into her drive. Frankie hadn't wanted to leave her car, a sweet little retro Thunderbird that suited her personality to a T, in the airport parking garage. Ross wasn't nearly so picky about his ten-year-old Jeep so he'd volunteered to drive.

A mountain of luggage sat on the front porch, causing him to slow as he made his way up her walk. She opened the door as he mounted the steps, another pair of gargantuan suitcases dragging at her arms. "Oh, good," she said, somewhat breathlessly. "You're here." She schlepped them to the growing pile. "I've got a couple more bags in the house. Would you mind getting them for me?"

Ross felt his eyes widen. He looked from her to the pile then back to her. "You have *more?*"

She straightened and set her hands at her waist. Her lips curled into that faint smile he'd love to kiss off. "Do we have to do this?" she asked. "It's *so* cliché."

Clichéd or not, who the hell needed this much stuff? Big bags, small bags, hat boxes. It was ridiculous. "How are you planning on getting all of this around?" he asked her. "Because unless Zora's hired you a personal luggage handler I foresee a major problem." He knew the instant the words left his mouth that he'd made a mistake. Ross squeezed his eyes shut and swore.

Frankie's ripe mouth slid into a happy smile and humor lit her dark chocolate gaze. "As a matter of fact, she has—you. *You* are my personal fetch-and-carry boy." She chuckled, cast a significant look at the luggage. "Mostly you'll be carrying."

Ross let go a small breath, trying his best to keep his patience. He'd decided that playing the whole burying-the-hatchet-in-each-other's-back game wouldn't serve either of them well on this trip. It was distracting under normal circumstances and these were hardly ordinary circumstances. In addition to his Duke of Desire duties—Ross inwardly shuddered at the title—he'd have to work as well. He couldn't afford to be any more distracted than he'd admittedly already be.

Frankie, damned her superior provoking hide, was distraction enough as it was.

He pushed a hand through his hair. "Are you absolutely sure you need all of this?"

She didn't even pretend to think about it. "All of this and what's left in the house."

Ross swallowed a long-suffering sigh. "Fine. Show me where the rest of it is."

Her lips formed the faintest of triumphant smiles as she led him into the house. "That's a good fetch-boy. Do well and I might actually tip you."

He'd show her a tip, Ross thought ominously, barely checking the impulse to respond. Furthermore, he was not a *boy*.

She shot him a curious look over her shoulder, evidently surprised that he didn't rise to the bait. "This way," she said, guiding him through her home. It was a traditional shotgun layout. Living room in front, kitchen, bed and bath. She'd maximized the small space by using lots of cool coastal colors, bead board and white furniture.

Which was why the bedroom came as a complete shock. Ross drew up short.

It was painted a deep royal purple. Purple velvet duvet, rich jewel-toned curtains and coordinating pillows. Huge mahogany bed and matching pieces. It was lush and feminine and...opulent. It was Kensington Palace meets courtesan boudoir. Tasteful, elegant, sensual and sexy. Frankie's particular scent hung in the air, a compelling combination of orange and ginger and his body immediately reacted. Heat singed his veins, settled in his loins and the fact that she—and a bed—were just a few mere feet away from him had belatedly registered in his lethargic brain.

Ross possessed one hell of an imagination— had to in his business—and it didn't take any effort on his part to imagine her naked body twisted in the white sheets and purple velvet.

Smooth bare legs, the vaguest curve of a breast peeking above the sheet, long gorgeous hair fanned out on a fluffy pillow...

Though he knew it was madness, Ross let the

vision continue, imagined himself sliding into bed with her…then sliding into her. Her mouth, usually rife with mockery, curled in invitation, her small cool hands smoothing over his skin. Touching him, enflaming him, making him—

Frankie gestured toward the luggage, cocked her head as though she knew precisely what was going on in his depraved head. "Are you waiting on them to sprout legs and *walk* to the car?"

Ross blinked, jerked from his musing and passed a hand over his burning face. Studiously avoiding her gaze, he mentally swore, then snagged the bags and made the return trip to the front porch. From there he began hauling her luggage to his car, her not lifting a finger but feeling compelled to direct him all the same.

"That's not going to fit there," she said, her voice just patronizing enough to make him want to scream. She pointed to another bag. "This one needs to go in first."

Ross expelled an irritated breath. The bury-the-hatchet game he'd sworn off was becoming increasingly harder to resist, but he absolutely refused to play. She might make him wretched, but he wasn't going to give her the satisfaction of knowing that she had, and he was going to be nice to her, get along with her—and ultimately thwart her—if it *freaking* killed him.

"I thought guys were supposed to be good at this," she said with a small *tsk*, clearly indicating that she was of the opinion that he was *not*. "Tell you what. Why don't you let me show you which ones to put where, and we'll get done with this a lot faster."

Which it probably would, he thought fatalistically.

Nevertheless, Ross pasted on a faltering, uncomfortable smile and despite the fact he desperately wanted to explain to her that it wasn't his packing skills that were in question, but rather a matter of physics—*no amount of arranging was going to make ten cubic feet of luggage fit in an eight-cubic-foot opening, dammit!*—he merely acquiesced. "Sure," he managed through slightly gritted teeth. "I'm open to suggestions."

For one split second she actually goggled at him, as though she couldn't believe he'd let her get away with being so unreasonable, but the look quickly vanished and soon she was pointing and gesturing like a music conductor. The only thing missing was the baton, which was best, he decided, because telling her to shove it up her delectable ass would have been intensely tempting.

In the end they wound up removing all of his own bags and allocating them to the luggage rack on the roof of his Jeep.

"Ah," she sighed maddeningly. "That's better, anyway, isn't it?"

Certainly, Ross thought. Picking the dead bugs off his luggage would give him something to do other than wring her neck.

Frankie dusted her hands, as though she'd actually contributed to the dirty work. "Let me make a quick run-through and make sure everything is off, take a bathroom break, and I'll be ready to go."

He nodded, followed her back inside and calmly waited for her in the living room. He passed the time by looking at framed photographs. There were several of her and her *Chicks-In-Charge* friends, snapshots of children he assumed were relatives, and a couple of a young boy who looked strikingly like Frankie.

That was odd, Ross thought with a slight frown. He could have sworn that he'd heard she was an only child.

He arched a brow as she walked back into the room. "You have a brother?" he asked.

She stopped and turned to stare at him. Her usually expressive gaze grew curiously shuttered. "No," she said tightly. "That's *me*."

Ross flushed at the gaffe, shoved his hands in his pockets. "Oh, sorry. It's just your hair..." Was hideous, he thought, daring to take a second look at one of the pictures. Why on earth had her mother butchered up her beautiful hair that way? he wondered. "Sorry," he repeated lamely.

"Don't be." Her lips curled with bitter humor. "Trust me. You aren't the only person who mistook me for a boy when I was that age." She mumbled something else just below his hearing, then slung her purse over her shoulder and waited by the door. "We should probably get going."

Still somewhat distracted, Ross blinked, then nodded and finally moved into action. "Right."

San Francisco

"A TWO BEDROOM suite?" Frankie parroted blankly.

"Yes, ma'am," the clerk behind the counter confirmed. She squinted at the computer screen. "You were in a single, but it looks like the reservation was upgraded last week. Double occupancy, two bedrooms." Smiling helpfully, the clerk gazed across the counter at Frankie, as though this was good news and she should be delighted. "Here are your room keys. Gerard—" she gestured to a bellhop waiting patiently with the two trolleys bearing their luggage "—will see you upstairs."

Frankie desperately wanted to argue, but a covert look from the corner of her eye told her that Ross wasn't any more pleased about this than she was—his distractingly handsome face wore a grim frown, one that she found distinctly unflattering—but that was the point, right? Frankie reminded herself glumly. Zora *wanted* him to be miserable. That's why she'd paired him up with her.

Evidently Ross had figured that out and absolutely—annoyingly—refused to play along. She'd taunted, teased, mocked and provoked at every opportunity since he'd arrived at her house this morning and, though she'd discerned a tic near his left eye and had actually heard his teeth grind, he'd been nothing but amiable and pleasant.

She hated it.

Ross fell into step behind her. "Nice hotel," he commented.

Frankie grunted, unable to come up with anything argumentative. She didn't mind being unkind to Ross, but there was no point in being purposely bitchy in front of the bellhop. After all, none of this was his fault.

It wasn't his fault that she'd sat next to Ross all the way out here and had been acutely, miserably aware of his arm brushing against hers.

It wasn't his fault that she'd spent more time covertly studying Ross's profile—the provocative curve of his mouth, specifically—and as a result of that minute scrutiny, she'd found herself so hot and bothered she'd squirmed in her seat for the better part of the flight.

It wasn't his fault that she'd barely refrained from tumbling Ross's marvelous ass into her bed this morning. Had barely refrained from conducting that infernal *interview* he'd alluded to during their lunch.

And it wasn't his fault that Ross had mistakenly taken her for a boy when he'd looked at her picture, thereby inadvertently opening an old wound that had never quite healed.

She'd *hated* that haircut, Frankie remembered as the old humiliation rolled through her. Her father—in another one of his hurtful attempts to turn her into the son he'd wanted but never had, she thought bitterly—had personally taken her to the barber shop and had her long, beautiful hair chopped off.

She'd quietly cried through the process, which had earned her one of the most brutal punishments she'd ever received. He'd whipped her for embarrassing him at the barber shop— for *crying like a little girl*—then whipped her harder when she'd sobbed through the pain. Cruel bastard. The best thing she'd ever done for herself was when she stopped trying to please him, when she'd walked out of the company and never looked back.

Frankie still spoke to her mother, but made it a point to make sure that her visits coincided with her father's frequent, usually lengthy *business trips*. She knew what sort of *business* he was conducting and, she thought with a grunt of disgust, it had nothing whatsoever to do with Salvaterra, Inc.

Ross helped Gerard maneuver their luggage up to their suite, and by the time they'd unloaded everything both of them had broken out into a mild sweat. She tipped Gerard handsomely and told Ross that his fly was open. It wasn't, of course, but she enjoyed watching his eyes widen and his hands grope for his zipper.

"Cute," he told her with a veiled smirk. "Very cute." He let go a long sigh and collapsed onto the couch in their shared sitting room. He rolled his head toward her, kicked his feet up onto the coffee table and crossed them at the ankles. "So, Girl Genius, what's next?"

Frankie ignored the way his jeans clung to his thighs, the way that his shirt molded to every muscled line, bump and rise of his abdomen and chest. Hell, who was she kidding? If she could *ignore* those things, her mouth wouldn't lose every ounce of moisture and her skin wouldn't feel too tight for her body. Her belly wouldn't clench with awareness every time those gorgeous eyes of his managed to tangle with hers, and she sure as hell wouldn't feel the foggy dew of joy juice seeping into her panties. Frankie resisted the urge to wail.

She couldn't ignore him. She'd tried.

The mind was *not* willing, the flesh was weak, and being in forced proximity with him for the next week would undoubtedly drive her insane. Her eyes narrowed. Particularly if he continued to be this amiable Joe that she didn't recognize.

Fighting with Ross, hurling insults, and giving tit for tat was her only form of release, the only way she managed to keep from throwing herself at his gorgeous body and begging him to take her to bed.

Or just take her.

Hell, she wasn't picky. A cozy linen closet, the back seat of his car, a bathroom stall. So long as she could feel every part of that hard body—including the hardest—beneath her fingers and deep inside her, then she wouldn't care.

Not until later, at which point she would be completely miserable, would be cursing her own stupidity and futilely wishing that she hadn't given into temptation.

Ross Hartford could break her heart.

She knew it. Had known it from the very beginning. Something about him called to her on a deeper level, something beyond the vein-singeing, spine-tingling attraction. What precisely, she didn't know, but in the grand scheme of things did it really matter? She didn't have to touch fire to know that she'd get burned. Ergo, she didn't have to sleep with Ross to know that she'd lose the ability to see reason and practice objectivity. To know that she'd become one of those pathetic morons who sacrificed their self-respect on the altar of true love.

As though to punctuate her thought, Ross's cell phone rang for at least the tenth time since they'd left this morning. Actually, he'd set it to vibrate, so it didn't ring, but she noted the incoming calls because he always unclipped the phone from his waist, then checked the display. And with the exception of one call he'd taken from his office, just like all the other times, he frowned and sent the caller to his voicemail.

Poor fool—or fools more likely—Frankie

thought, wondering if it was maybe the bouquet-sender he'd just neatly dismissed. She shook her head and felt a disgusted, knowing smirk slide across her lips. If she slept with him, that could just as easily be her.

Her he didn't speak to. *Her* he sent to voice-mail. *Her* he made wretched.

Ha. She'd sew her legs closed with a rusty knitting needle first.

She *wouldn't* sleep with him, he *wouldn't* break her heart, and she *was not* going to let him be nice to her—the outcome would only be disastrous.

For her.

5

ROSS TOOK THE OPPORTUNITY to call home and check on things while Frankie freshened up and changed out of her traveling clothes. Their first appearance was in just under an hour, but luckily they wouldn't be required to travel beyond the hotel for this one. The PR firm Zora had hired to handle the launch had booked one of the larger meeting rooms, and from the looks of things they'd done a bang-up job. He'd noticed several *CHiC* banners and advertisements when they'd come into the hotel. The word was out. It would be interesting to see just how many people turned up.

Though he knew he should be nervous— aside from extensive practical experience, he really didn't have any idea how to dole out sex advice—frankly, being *CHiC*'s Duke of Desire was the least of his problems.

The realization that he'd be practically sharing a room with Frankie had taken the top spot on his worry list.

From the beginning, something about Zora and Tate's bet—about his and Frankie's unfortunate part in it, specifically—had seemed... off...to Ross. Like he'd pointed out to Frankie, Zora had lost and yet she'd still seemed particularly pleased. It hadn't made any sense then, but with the advent of the essentially shared room, things had begun to get a little clearer.

Zora was matchmaking.

Could he prove it? No. Would he mention his suspicions to Frankie? Hell, no. He'd grown rather fond of breathing—of living, in particular—and she'd undoubtedly go for his throat.

Ross felt a faint grin tug at his lips. Honestly, though, he was quite surprised that she hadn't put it together yet. Knowing how that keen mind worked, Ross figured Zora must have done one helluva snow job to so thoroughly pull the wool over her eyes.

That or the idea of them getting together was so far removed from her thinking that it simply wouldn't occur to her.

Ross immediately dismissed the curiously disturbing thought. In the past he'd detected enough heat in that dark-as-sin gaze to suggest that he wasn't locked in this perverse attraction alone, but being with her today had gratifyingly confirmed it. She'd stared at his mouth so long he'd been hard-pressed not to lean over and kiss her. His loins felt like they'd been left under a hot light for the entire friggin' flight, and he'd entertained himself by imagining the two of them inducting the hell out of each other into the Mile High Club.

In addition to that, Ross had invented a new way to keep from fighting with her. Every time she spewed a stream of sarcastic acid at him, or lobbed an insult, he merely smiled at her and thought of another way to take her.

In his mind's eye, he'd had her on her back, on her knees, on her belly, against a wall, in a shower, on top, on bottom, on her head and a few other positions he was relatively sure were anatomically impossible, and if not, then most likely banned by the Church.

He could tell that it was absolutely infuriating her that he wouldn't argue—in addition to staring at his mouth, she'd spent a great deal of the time alternately bitching, huffing and rolling her eyes—which, naturally, increased his fun. In fact, he wished he'd thought to do this a long time ago. Being around her would have been a great deal simpler.

Nevertheless, he thought grimly, there was a fly in the ointment.

Thinking about all the ways he'd love to land between her legs left him even more—though he wouldn't have thought it possible—sexually frustrated than before.

Also, while he should have taken his time on the flight here to review his notes and work, the Maxwell account had been the furthest thing from his mind. He hadn't given it a single thought because every cell in *both* his heads had been consumed with thoughts of Frankie. This didn't bode well, Ross thought grimly. Not well at all.

"You aren't going to change?"

Ross looked up. Shit. He'd forgotten. "I—"

"Oh, it's just as well," she said with a smile that was at least two parts cream. "You're supposed to wear this." She tossed a shirt at him.

Ross caught it, then held it up. He felt his expression blacken and an immediate, "Hell, no!" formed on his tongue.

"Isn't it nice?" Frankie goaded sweetly. She crossed her arms over her chest and gleefully waited for him to lose his temper.

Using visual therapy, he imagined hooking her legs over his shoulders and miraculously kept it in check. Ross pushed a brittle smile into place and tilled the barren field of his black mind for something charitable to say about the shirt. "One hundred percent cotton," he finally managed. "And preshrunk."

Apparently, that was the last straw. Frankie's eyes narrowed in irritation and her nostrils flared as she dragged in a harsh breath. She grew a couple of inches, which, coupled with the heels put her at five and half feet. *"That's it?"* she all but shrieked. The sleek ponytail she'd pulled her hair into wobbled threateningly and a wash of angry color flooded her cheeks. "It's hot pink with the *Chicks-In-Charge* logo, the bloody Duke of Desire blazing across it…and that's all you have to say? That's its one hundred percent cotton and preshrunk?" Her voice climbed with every syllable, making it extremely difficult for him to keep a straight face.

"You're right," Ross said, trying to look properly chastised. He belatedly conjured a gracious smile. "Thank you."

She stared at him for a moment, then actually growled low in her throat. He got the distinct impression she would have liked to stamp her foot. "Just get ready," she finally said, practically chewing the words from between gritted teeth. "We have to be downstairs in a few minutes."

Ross nodded. "I'll hurry," he promised accommodatingly, knowing it would grate against her nerves. With another dark look and a couple of words that sounded suspiciously like "screw you," she turned and walked out of the room.

FRANKIE SHOT a furtive look toward her bedroom door, then cupped her hand over the receiver. "This is not working," she whispered vehemently into the phone.

"What are you talking about?" Zora replied, a frown in her voice. "You haven't even started yet." She drew a breath and when she spoke again lead laced her voice. "Did the PR people not do their job because I will flat let them—"

"No. No, no, no," Frankie interrupted. "I'm talking about Ross," she wailed quietly. "This is not working. I—I can't do this."

Zora paused and when she spoke a curious, unreadable note rang in her voice. "Do what specifically?"

Frankie flung herself onto the edge of the bed. "Get along with him. He's driving me crazy!"

"How so? You just got there."

Logical questions, Frankie knew, but she wasn't thinking logically. Hell, she wasn't thinking at all. How could she when with every passing second she wanted him more?

"Look," Frankie said, her voice weary and throbbing even to her own ears. "You paired him up with me to make him unhappy—and it's… It's not working. He refuses to argue with me. He won't fight with me. I have bossed him around, made him haul my luggage and I just played my trump card—*the shirt*—and he merely smiled and said 'thank you.' Your plan isn't working, so I want you to call it off. Put him to work at the office. Have him— Have him clean out the gutters, scrub toilets or some other menial degrading task you're sure he won't like. I don't care." She blew out a harsh breath, gestured tiredly. "Just get him away from me."

Before I do something stupid, Frankie thought. *Like sleep with him.*

Silence pulsed over the line, then, "Let me get this straight. You want me to undo all of the work I've done to put him on board with this tour—call every city and yank him from the schedule—just because he's being *nice* to you?"

Frankie blinked. She realized that to rational-thinking people it probably sounded petulant and insane, but... "Yes, that's exactly what I want."

"Well, you can forget it," Zora returned flatly. "Frankie, this is ridiculous. What's wrong with him being nice to you? What's so bad about that?"

Zora was one of her very best friends, but there was no way in hell she could explain it. One, Zora would read too much into it. Two, Zora would tell Tate, who would in turn tell Ross, and then he'd know that she was miserably horny for him and she'd be humiliated and looking for the nearest hole to fall into. She'd be mortified. Irritated and miserable was a much more palatable combination than mortified and miserable.

"Nothing, I suppose. But I thought my mission was to make him miserable. Isn't that why you put him with me? To make sure that he didn't enjoy himself?" That still stung, dammit. She was more accustomed to being a pleasure than a punishment.

"Well, if fighting with him isn't working, then I suggest you try something else."

Frankie snorted. "Like what?"

A long-suffering sigh sounded in her ear. "Frankie, there are other ways of making a man...miserable than merely arguing with him. You're a woman and our Carnal Contessa to boot. Figure it out."

Frankie inhaled sharply as understanding dawned. "If you are suggesting that I—"

"He's hot for you. Think about it. I'm getting another call...bye."

And she was gone. Frankie gaped and stared at the receiver. Zora had hung up on her! Had dropped a bomb like that…and then simply just hung up on her.

What the hell was she talking about? *He was hot for her?* What would make her— Frankie's heart misfired. Had Tate told her that? she wondered with a startled gasp. Her belly did an odd little roll, not altogether unpleasant. Granted there'd been times when she'd caught a flash of heat in those curiously compelling eyes, the occasional prickle of awareness, as though he'd been looking at her and she'd just missed it. Frankie paused, considering. She supposed it could be possible, but—

He rapped on her door frame. "I'm ready."

Jerked from her thoughts, Frankie looked up and her lips twitched. Was it her imagination, or did he sound a wee bit grim? She crossed her arms over her chest. "It's a fetching shade, wouldn't you say?"

With a fleeting look of distaste, he plucked the shirt away from his body. She watched him struggle to push his lips into a smile. "It's… It's eye-catching."

"I'm glad you like it."

"Making you happy is my greatest wish," he told her.

There was an edge to his voice that suggested otherwise, but the comment drew a shiver deep from her womb. She knew beyond a shadow of a doubt that Ross Hartford could make her happy in places that hadn't so much as smiled in months.

For reasons beyond her immediate understanding, she'd been loathe to take a new lover. She'd been fixated on Ross—on what it would be like to have sex with Ross, specifically—and the idea of being with someone else smacked of a substitute.

Until she could get over this unholy attraction, she'd tend to her own needs. She mentally shrugged. Not as satisfying as the genuine article, she knew, but a little relief was better than none, and it was comforting to know that she wasn't dependent on a man for the benefit of an orgasm.

Frankly, she didn't like being dependent on a man for anything. Wouldn't ever be, if she could help it.

Furthermore, she couldn't help but feel a bit

sorry for those women who didn't indulge in knowing their bodies. Just another double standard she hoped to change through her work with the magazine and *Chicks-In-Charge*. Hell, when boys hit puberty they were expected to masturbate, were counseled even on the naturalism of their budding sexuality.

Girls were given the so-called "talk"—if they were lucky, she thought with a mental snort, recalling her own horrid experience—and could expect to bleed, bloat and cramp for the next forty plus years. How fair was that? Why was it natural for boys to experiment, but girls were made to feel dirty or strange for indulging in the same behavior?

Considering most guys could climax when the wind blew the right way and women typically needed a bit more skilled stimulation, it would seem better for both sexes if a woman learned from the beginning what sort of touch she responded to. For a woman to know her body well enough to discern what was going to trip her trigger.

The victims of ripening hormones and poor education, too many young girls in search of some sort of release were squandering their virginity on boys who knew how to find their own pleasure, but were sorely lacking the finesse to see to their partner.

Her gaze drifted to Ross and she pulled in a small quivering breath. She instinctively knew *that* wouldn't be the case with Ross. There were some guys a woman simply knew would be good in bed, would live up to the hype of their sexuality.

Ross was one of those guys.

It was a million different little things, insignificant on their own, but when combined with the rest made for one helluva package.

It was the way he moved, confident and unhurried, lazy yet purposeful. There was a secret knowledge in that heavy-lidded gaze that promised pleasure and invited sin, an unconcerned intensity that went beyond the average sex appeal.

It was more than nice lips or excellent bone structure. More than strong sensual hands and that certain way he cocked his head when he looked at her. Everything about Ross Hartford did it for her. Made her belly tremble and her thighs quake. Made her palms itch and her sex quicken.

Ordinarily Frankie could find fault with a guy. There'd be one little thing that turned her off or made her wince. Ugly feet, fat earlobes, hairy knuckles. Shallow, yes, but she couldn't help herself. But if Ross had an imperfection, she hadn't found it yet and, disturbingly, she imagined if she did find one, it, too, would be sexy. Frankie let go a small sigh and resigned herself to being a sexually frustrated wreck for the duration of their acquaintance. Translate, *the rest of her misbegotten life.*

With that sobering thought, she reluctantly got to her feet. It was time to go tell other people how to achieve sexual happiness. With an imperious wave she knew he would hate, Frankie motioned for Ross to come along.

Wearing the loud shirt and a distinctly grim smile, Ross obligingly followed her downstairs. "Is there a particular theme in mind?" he asked. "Or are you just going to take questions and wing it?"

"Actually, a little of both. We'll start by talking about chemistry, what makes a person attractive to another person and all that, then move into foreplay. Kissing, massage." Frankie swallowed. She couldn't think about those things without factoring Ross into the picture. "Beyond that, we'll talk about what makes a good lover, and then we'll take questions."

Ross cleared his throat. "And that's where I'll come in, right?"

Was it her imagination or did he sound a smidge…nervous? She felt her lips twitch. "What happened to you being an expert? Having loads of experience and references and all that? Won't you want to add the male perspective to what I've already got?"

Ross held the elevator door, allowing her to exit first. She dimly noted the dull roar of excited conversation. "I've read your articles," he drawled lazily. "You seem to have a pretty good grasp of your…subject."

An unexpected flush of pleasure washed through her, loosening her limbs, and a slow smile crept up the corners of her mouth. "You've read my articles?"

"Every last one." He shot her a droll, considering look. "Don't let this go to your head, but you're very good. Knowledgeable and funny. It's no wonder your column has been such a success, or why Zora chose you to headline this launch."

Frankie blinked, unaccustomed to the praise. She was in no danger of letting his assessment go to her head, but the compliment lodged directly into her heart and suffused her body with a ridiculous amount of pleasure. She was used to being complimented by men on her looks and…other talents, but she'd never received any sort of praise regarding her work. Frankie mentally harrumphed. God knows her father had never tossed out any compliments for a job well-done or otherwise.

A harried-looking woman armed with a walkie-talkie and clipboard hurried forward as they approached the banquet hall. "Ms. Salvaterra?"

Frankie nodded and shook the woman's hand. "That's me." She gestured to Ross. "And this is Ross Hartford, our honorary Duke of Desire." From the corner of her eye she watched Ross flinch. Frankie resisted the urge to rock back on her heels.

"Excellent," the woman replied. "I'm Treva Kline with Grant Media PR. The room is ready and—" she smiled and canted her head toward the ever-increasing noise "—you're talking to a packed house. We ended up removing another partition and called up another hundred chairs. They're a…" Her smile wobbled. "They're a lively crowd."

Another hundred chairs? Frankie thought, slightly amazed. She'd expected a full room. They'd planned the tour based on the highest ISP hits from the Web site, but another hundred chairs above what they'd planned? Zora would definitely be pleased.

"You should probably head on in," Treva suggested as the din hit a particularly loud note. "The, uh… The natives sound restless. Good luck."

Anticipation spiked. Frankie put her hand on the doorknob, looked back over her shoulder at Ross and smiled. "I'm not going to need any luck. But you are."

6

AND SHE WAS undoubtedly right, Ross thought as Frankie, looking completely in her element, swung open the doors and marched through. Salt-N-Pepa's "Let's Talk About Sex" blared from large speakers set onstage. The entire room vaulted from their seats and went wild. *CHiC* magazines—which had evidently been handed out as guests came into the room—were being waved like flags. Women catcalled, clapped, screamed and whistled, and several more industrious souls had made banners and were currently standing on the chairs.

In short, it was *wild,* and though some might believe it was sacrilegious to compare the two, Ross was strongly reminded of Beatlemania. These women certainly liked their sex tips, he thought with a somewhat uneasy laugh as he trailed behind in Frankie's wake.

Rather than being intimidated by the crowd, Frankie seemed to thrive on it. Confidence straightened her spine and she moved through the pressing group as though she owned it. She laughed delightedly, smiled and waved, and along with just the faintest hint of hesitant joy, there was a distinct glimmer of pride in those gorgeous dark brown eyes.

Ross felt a smile flirt with the corner of his mouth. Reading Frankie's column, one could easily deduce that she loved her job—it was evident in every word, by the simple tongue-in-cheek way she crafted her articles.

But this went well beyond merely loving her job, he thought as he watched her mount the steps to the stage and move toward the microphone. There was an intensity, a passion behind her work that one didn't often see.

She *believed* in what she was doing, he realized, and for that he both admired and envied her.

While he'd always worked hard to be the best—*had to be the best because anything less was wholly unacceptable*—Ross could honestly admit that convincing people to buy things they didn't particularly need wasn't exactly a life-changing, noble career. His lips quirked. He supposed choosing one brand of deodorant over another might be life-changing to some, but he sincerely doubted it.

Until he'd read her columns Ross wouldn't have thought that doling out lovemaking advice to a bunch of undersexed housewives, quivering virgins and the orgasmically-challenged would have been life-changing either, but the message behind Frankie's advice was always the same—independence. Be it learning to take matters into your own hands, so to speak—the idea drew a smile—or drumming up the nerve to gently critique a lousy lover, the message remained true voice your needs, take control, gain independence.

Be a door *opener*, not a door*mat*.

His gaze slid to where she stood behind the podium and a curious sense of pride—misplaced, of course, if she ever found out about it—swelled in his chest, forcing him to exhale a small sigh.

Frankie gazed out over the room and waited for the music to fade and for everyone to take their seats before speaking. "Wow," she finally breathed, wide-eyed and happy. "I see that you all received your new magazines."

This statement was met with a deafening roar of approval from the group.

Frankie chuckled softly. "So I guess it's safe to say that you approve of the new format, eh?"

Another peal of laughter and applause echoed through the room.

"And—" Frankie tapped her finger against her chin, an exaggerated look of innocent concentration on her beautiful face "—I wonder what you want to talk about."

Let's talk about sex, baby! Let's talk about you and me! Let's talk about sex, baby...

The pop song's refrain played a couple more times, once again working the crowd into a frenzy of anticipation. Ross shook his head. And men were supposed to be obsessed with dipping their wicks? Were continually ridiculed for thinking with their dicks? This was... This was...enlightening, Ross finally decided as he gazed with blatant wonder at the crowd. Evidently women were just as interested in getting it—or better yet, getting it *good*—as men were. At least this particular group was.

"Okay," Frankie continued when the throng had once again found their seats. "I know why you're here and we're not going to disappoint you. We're gonna talk about sex." She smiled grimly. "The good, the bad, and the ugly. And—" she looked meaningfully at Ross "—as an added bonus, you're not only going to hear from me on the subject—you're going to get the male perspective."

More catcalling, more whistling and a couple of distinct ooh-la-la's resonated through the room. Ross felt the tips of his ears burn and he was suddenly hit with the overwhelming urge to flee. He told himself that he wasn't afraid, especially not of a group of horny women, dammit—geez, how friggin' degrading—and firmly rooted himself to the floor.

"This is Ross Hartford, *CHiC*'s official Duke of Desire for this tour." She slid him a sly glance. "According to Ross, he's an *expert* when it comes to sex—has had loads of experience," she added meaningfully. "So feel free to ask him *any* question you'd like. I'm sure he'll be able to answer you."

The evil smile Frankie wore as she imparted his introduction and qualifications was downright gleeful. To his complete irritation and astonishment, he felt even more heat rise in his face.

Ross pushed his lips up into a shadow of a smile and pretended that he didn't want to throttle her. But they both knew better. She was getting to him again, and the idea that he was actually letting her braced him more than anything else could. Did he want to talk about sex with a room full of strangers? Hell, no. Did he want to talk about—and more importantly, have sex—with Frankie? Hell, yes.

So that's what he would focus on, Ross decided, strengthened by the idea of a plan. Whenever he answered a question, he'd think about her. What *she* would like. What would turn *her* on. How he could wind her up, then lead her to release. His own personal toy, he thought, warming to his idea. Warming, period. He shifted uncomfortably. In places that it would become completely obvious if he didn't get control of himself. Sheesh. He was going to need professional help by the time this was over with. Medication and a straitjacket.

Though it took every ounce of willpower he possessed, Ross sent her a smile, one that promised unknown retribution and he had the pleasure of watching the slightest bit of trepidation flash in that too perceptive gaze.

Though he could tell he'd rattled her, Frankie recovered well and launched into her welcome speech, covered the goals of the magazine and plugged *Chicks-In-Charge* as a whole. "If you haven't joined a local chapter, I would encourage you to do so. Women are nurturers and bonders. Who better than to help our own cause than mothers, daughters, wives? And ex-wives," she added with a wry smile. "We all have something to offer, and the benefits of being a part of a group that encourages every sort of independence is..." Frankie paused, struggled to find the right word. "It's amazing," she finally finished. "I—I can't tell you how it's changed my life."

There was a touching wealth of conviction in her voice, a truth that was heard and felt by every person in the room, himself included.

Just what exactly was so wrong with her life, Ross wondered, that *Chicks-In-Charge* had been able to fix? He vaguely remembered Tate talking about Frankie's father, but Zora had given her husband a sharp look, one that to Ross's disappointment had instantly shut him up.

His gaze inexplicably moved to her face, the sweet but stubborn curve of her cheek, and a funny sensation—one he instinctively didn't try to name—winged through his chest. He was suddenly hit with the urge to know all of her secrets, to right her wrongs. A new inkling of understanding hit him between the eyes, giving him a sense of vision he hadn't known in the past. *He saw it now.* Hell, didn't know why he hadn't seen it before, or how he could have missed it in the first place, but…she'd been hurt.

Deeply.

Ross stilled. The you-can't-touch-me attitude, the sword of sarcasm she wielded with uncanny precision… It was all there, now that he could actually take a moment to look. Before he'd been too blinded by the attraction, by the sheer force of her presence, and the sleight-of-hand magic show of her performance to see it.

But he saw it now…which was bad for her because Ross wouldn't be satisfied until he knew all of her little secrets, every detail she'd carefully—painstakingly—kept hidden.

Though he had no idea where the notion came from—and instinctively knew that she'd equally deny and resent it—Ross had the oddest impression that Frankie Salvaterra needed something and, for reasons which escaped his immediate understanding, he *knew* he was the only guy who could give it to her. What was this mysterious something? He let go a breath. Hell, who knew? But the knowledge was there, an indefinable gut instinct that was as elusive as air, but just as real, all the same.

Frankie jabbed him with a manicured nail, startling him out of his reverie. "Hey, Dick of Desire," she muttered under her breath with a feigned smile toward the room at large. "Someone just asked you a question. Are you going to answer her, or stand here looking like a handsome half-wit all day?"

Ross cocked his head toward hers, inexplicably pleased with the backhanded compliment. "You think I'm handsome?"

Still wearing a brittle grin, she snorted under her breath. "Did you miss the half-wit part?"

"No, I didn't miss it. I chose to ignore it."

"Half-wits usually do. Answer her question," she ordered tightly. "You're making us look like fools."

"Ah, well," he sighed without the least bit of contrition. "I guess Zora should have thought about that before making me come on this trip."

"Given that you're usually conscientious about your work, I'm sure that it never occurred to her that you wouldn't try to do your best."

Ross grinned and pretended to swoon. "Handsome and conscientious? This is definitely a red-letter day. Better be careful or all this praise is going to go to my head." The wrong one, he mentally added.

"Now that would be tragic. I don't see how you haul that thing around on your shoulders as it is."

"I work out," Ross told her with mock humility.

An irritated huff poofed past her lips and her eyes widened. "For the love of God, just answer the question."

The hint of desperation in her voice was particularly gratifying. "Yes, well. Here's the rub. In order for me to answer the question, *dearest*, I first have to know what it is."

Instead of simply telling him herself, Frankie leaned closer to the microphone. "Sorry, ladies," she drawled with a pointed look in his direction. "Our Duke of Desire is wearing his *thong* a little too tight and evidently it's cutting off the circulation to his *brain*." She smiled sweetly and gestured toward a woman seated on the front row. "Could you please repeat your question?"

His thong was cutting off the circulation to his brain? Ross thought darkly. Meaning his head was up his ass, he wondered, or that his brain was in his dick? He grimaced. Either way, it was not a flattering assessment. But apparently a funny one. The entire room guffawed at his expense and Frankie, damn her delectable hide, looked distinctly pleased with herself. What he'd give to wipe that smug smile off her face...

The woman with the question finally spoke up, snagging his attention. "I just wondered if the Duke had any suggestions on how to clean up a sloppy kisser." She rolled her eyes. "My husband nearly drowns me. By the time we're finished making love, I need more than a towel—I need a wet-vac."

The comment drew a laugh from his own throat as well as from around the room. Ross glanced over to share the humor with Frankie only to discover that her ripe mouth had lost its usual smirk and that her gaze had once again— provokingly—dropped to his mouth. A blast of heat detonated in his loins and his fingers literally itched to trace the familiar slope of her cheek. Jesus, didn't she have any idea what that was doing to him? Didn't she realize that she couldn't stare at his mouth without him thinking about attaching it to hers? Didn't she—

Ross grew utterly still as an epiphany of perfect proportions unfurled in his whirling brain. His own gaze dropped to her mouth—to that plump bottom lip, the very one he'd imagined suckling too many times to count. His heart all but stopped, then galloped back into motion, and the room around them seemed to fade to black.

He watched her eyes widen in recognition of his plan, in what he was about to do and caught the vaguest perception of a shake of her head. He sidled closer to her.

"Actually, ma'am, the best defense for a sloppy kisser is to teach them a new technique. Our Carnal Contessa here previously agreed to submit to any demonstrations—"

Her eyes widened and flashed fire. "No, I didn't. I—"

"Oh, come on, now," he cajoled, moving close enough into her personal space to discern the fluttering pulse point in her neck. He laced her fingers through his and pulled her closer with a determined tug. "We're here to educate, right? Isn't that what you're all about?" He smiled down into her somewhat panicked eyes.

"I don't think—"

"See, ladies," Ross lamented with a shake of his head. He wrapped an arm around her waist, hauling her fully up against him. "That's part of the problem. Women put too much thinking into the process. It's really very simple." He cupped her jaw with one hand, watched her lids briefly close beneath his touch before she managed to wrench them open again. "Before a man should kiss a woman, he should establish physical contact, make sure that she's ready for it." His eyes tangled with hers. "That she's anticipating his next move. His very taste." She blinked drunkenly at him, absently licked her lips, inadvertently kicking his heart rate into overdrive. What was he doing again? Oh, yeah... "Then, once he realizes that she's not averse to his advances, he should gently brush his lips over hers. Like this." Ross held eye contact until he could feel the sweet fan of her breath against his mouth, then shaking slightly, he sighed and ever so gently skimmed his lips across hers.

The first shock of contact stole the breath from his lungs, made every hair on his body stand on end, made his knees quiver.

Sweet Jesus...

He drew back and looked at her, noted her equally shaken expression. "Then, once he's made that initial move, he should gradually increase the pressure, up the tempo." Following his own advice, he fitted his lips over hers again. Once, twice, felt her shudder, tasted a reluctant mewl of pleasure. "Finding that perfect point between wet and dry is a bit of an art, but it can be done. It's all in the tongue. Too much is sloppy, too little too dry." He let go a shaky breath. "In any case, practice makes perfect." He slid his hand around to the back of her neck, angled her head for better access, then laid a full siege against her mouth.

Ross vaguely noted a roar of applause as his mouth fully melded with hers. Hell's own angels could have materialized out of thin air and he doubted he would have noticed.

Kissing Frankie absolutely consumed him.

Cognitive thinking short-circuited beneath the frenetic melting heat tasting her wrought. She was darkness and light, sin and salvation, and stopping at a mere kiss was going to be the most difficult thing he'd ever have to do.

Thankfully, after the first brush of his lips against hers, she'd given up any pretense of resistance—had draped her arms around his neck and sagged against him. Her lush form— soft breasts, taut nipples—molded seamlessly with his, as though a divine hand had crafted her expressly for him. A blast of heat lodged in his loins, steamed him up from the inside out, and a quivery sensation borne of an emotion he dare not name commenced in his gut.

Frankie's tongue chased a sigh into his mouth, curled around his with inherent skill, and skimmed the sensitive inside of his cheek, his own personal On button. A tingle shivered down his spine. Every suckle and slide of her lips pushed him that much closer to an edge he'd been skating for months, and though he was loathe to call an end to their kiss, he knew he had to. The room which had gone curiously quiet had once again resumed making noise—catcalls, whistles and pointed *ahem-ahem's.*

Ross framed her face once more, slid the pad of his thumb along her cheekbone, then very gently ended the kiss. Her gaze was dark with passion, with a secret knowledge he wasn't privy to and just the smallest hint of foregone despair. He particularly identified with the latter, with the uncomfortable truth of what it revealed—one kiss would *never* be enough.

A single taste could *never* satisfy his hunger.

Frankie was the fever and the cure, the ache and the relief…the ultimate yin to his yang.

His death wish, Ross remembered with a fatalistic smile, but oh, what a way to go.

7

HE'D KISSED HER.

Frankie shrugged out of her robe, tested the water with her toe and, deeming it okay, stepped into the whirlpool tub and sank beneath the steaming, scented water. *When in doubt, bathe,* she thought with a tired, still-tingling smile.

And right now she had several doubts—doubts about her sanity, in particular—because letting Ross kiss her—then melting all over him and kissing him back—could only mean that she'd lost her freakin' mind. She whimpered and groaned, banged her head against the back of the tub. There was absolutely no other excuse for her mortifying—thrilling—behavior. Hours later she still couldn't wrap her mind around it, couldn't recall ever being so affected by a kiss.

One minute she'd been quietly chortling over

his displeasure, and the next she'd looked up and caught that calculating, predatory gleam in his eye…and she'd instantly known what he'd planned to do. Could see it just as plainly as if he'd said, "Brace yourself, baby, because I'm about to rock your world."

And he had.

He'd shaken her to the core, to the very foundation of her soul. There'd been something erotically thrilling listening to him broadcast his every move, feeling that warm palm connect in a gentle gesture of affection against her cheek. Frankie was used to being wanted. Men frequently wanted her. She paused, reliving the moment when Ross's hand had caressed her face.

But there was something altogether different about the way he'd touched her. There was a sweetness, for a lack of better explanation—a fondness of feeling—behind the sensual touch which had taken her off guard. It had made the back of her throat tighten, made a rogue wave of joy bolt through her. Then, before she'd had time to battle it back, or label it something else—a handy little tool of denial she'd mastered over the years—he'd leaned forward and brushed his lips against hers...and she'd been lost.

Utterly and completely lost.

Fortunately, he'd managed to maintain a small amount of reason and had ended the kiss before either one of them could do something even more ignorant—like peeling their clothes off and doing it right there in front of a roomful of people. Frankie chuckled. *That* would have been a demonstration they definitely wouldn't have forgotten anytime soon.

Getting back on track afterward had been damned difficult, and only by promising herself that she could evaluate the whole episode to her heart's content once she was back in her room did she manage to pull it all together.

Luckily, they'd both regained a portion of their senses and had tried to put a professional spin on the so-called lips-on lesson, but no one had been fooled, least of all, she was sure, the audience.

She'd practically staggered from the force of his kiss, and Ross's *royal staff* had made a prominent tent in the front of his trousers. That, of course, was as gratifying as it was frustrating. Gratifying because eliciting that sort of a reaction from a guy that quickly was something to preen about—frustrating because she knew she couldn't have it.

Kissing Ross was one thing—making a lover out of him was another, and she would fight that natural—almost   overwhelming—transition with every horny, miserable fiber of her being.

He'd ruin her. He'd break her heart. Everything she'd worked hard to do, to maintain— namely, her self-respect—would be burned up and consumed by him and the feelings he managed to effortlessly evoke.

Until Ross had come along, Frankie had fancied herself untouchable. She'd never met a guy who could shake her, who could make her forget that men were untrustworthy, unfaithful bastards. Oh, she'd certainly liked a few guys, had developed a small amount of affection for them. But there'd always been a part of her that held back, that she kept just for herself. That remained her own.

Ross, she knew, could take that part because, without the smallest bit of effort on his behalf, she'd gladly hand it over. She knew she would. Ross Hartford was different. She'd felt it from the very beginning, recognized the fact that he was a threat from the first instant those compelling eyes had collided with hers.

If she made love to Ross—or better yet, he made love to her the way she knew he could—she'd want things she'd never wanted from another guy. Exclusive rights. Undying love. A faithful partner. A humorless smile curled her lips. The stuff of fairy tales.

Did she wish things were different? Most definitely. On a purely physical level she wanted him more than she'd ever wanted another man. Heat flashed in her nipples and buzzed her neglected sex. Her blood chugged slowly in her veins, making her belly flutter with unrelieved tension. Her mind obligingly called up acts of depravity she'd love to reenact in the flesh.

Her palms mapping his chest… His mouth latched on to her aching nipple, then her weeping sex… His hands spanning her waist as she deliberately—painstakingly—rode him to climax. Frankie's breath left her in a stuttering whoosh and another quivering arrow of heat found its mark between her legs. She bit her lip, rolled her head to the side and whimpered.

Oh, God, how was she going to do this? How was she supposed to spend the rest of the week with him and not give in? Not have him?

Frankie heaved herself out of the tub, clumsily dried off, then wrapped her body in one of the fluffy hotel robes. The terry cloth abraded her sensitive nipples, pulling another woebegone whimper of frustration from her throat. She opened the bathroom door and, from her vantage point as she made her way into her bedroom, she caught a glimpse of Ross's bare feet propped up on their sitting-room table. She caught the faint ticking of keys, meaning that he'd pulled his laptop out and, instead of fantasizing about having sex—like her, dammit—he'd easily sat down and shifted into work mode.

"Frankie?" he called out, still clicking away.

"Yes."

"April called while you were in the tub. Her call-back number is on the pad next to your bed."

April had called? Frankie frowned, immediately wondering if something had gone wrong. April was currently in the middle of a huge redesign on the site. With the advent of the glossy format, the board had decided that something really cool needed to be in place on the Web. They anticipated a small decline in Web hits once the new look hit the stands, but wanted to be able to pull those readers back as well.

In order to achieve that goal, there had to be something unique to offer the reader in each venue. April, their creative guru, was heading up the project.

Concerned that something might have gone wrong, or that she needed her input, Frankie muttered a distracted thanks to Ross, then made her way to her room and returned the call.

April answered on the second ring. "Hello."

"Hey, it's Frankie. Ross mentioned that you'd called. Is everything all right?"

"Oh, yeah, it's fine," April replied breezily. "I just had some good news I thought you'd be interested in hearing."

A smile rolled around her lips. "You got your orgasm back?"

"Er...no."

"Damn," Frankie winced. For reasons no one could begin to fathom, April had gone from enjoying a healthy, satisfying sex life to…nothing. No amount of stimulation—self-inflicted or otherwise—could bring her to climax. She'd recently taken up kick-boxing to relieve some of the stress, but Frankie could tell that her situation was really beginning to wear on her.

Hell, Frankie had been celibate for months, too, but at least she'd managed to see to her own needs. Thus far nothing she'd suggested that April try had worked and, other than one last-ditch idea, she assumed April had given them all a fair shot. There was no help for it, Frankie decided. April was going to have to call him.

"You've tried that last technique I told you about?" she asked, just for clarification.

April's sigh hissed over the line. "I did."

"Then you know what I think. Call him."

She could feel her friend's hesitation over the line. "If it comes to that," she hedged.

Frankie chuckled. "Honey, if you ever want to *come* again, you're going to have to call him.

He's a clit mechanic…and from what I've heard knows exactly how to make a woman purr. He can fix you," she insisted. Frankie chuckled. "Hell, he's not called the Vagina Whisperer for nothing."

Ben Hayes, the last-ditch idea in question, was a quintessential bad boy, a guy from the so-called wrong side of the tracks who thumbed his nose at the middle class, hated the idle rich and showed his disdain by competently seducing any girl he supposedly couldn't have, usually one already attached or engaged to a guy belonging to one of the aforementioned groups. He was a legendary lover, another fix-me male, and had left more than one broken heart in his wake.

Which was undoubtedly why April was hesitant to seek his particular brand of expertise. Furthermore, on the rare occasions Ben had hung with their group, Frankie had sensed a certain…chemistry/history between the two. There was a story there, but until April was ready to share, she'd simply have to keep her speculations to herself.

"We'll see," April said. "Anyway, the reason

I called was because I wanted to let you know how well your session went this afternoon."

Frankie frowned. How could she tell how well her session had gone? She wasn't—

April's voice vibrated with excitement. "I've gotten *tons* of e-mail this afternoon and the boards are bogged down with dozens of posts, all of them touting what a fantastic time—and what a fantastic pair—" she emphasized delightedly "—you and Ross make. Apparently, there was some to-do about a kissing demonstration?" she asked leadingly.

Frankie's stomach flip-flopped. Oh, hell. She cleared her throat. "Er…that's right. One of the attendants asked Ross how to fix a sloppy kisser and he decided that a…that a demonstration would best answer the question."

April squealed delightedly. "Ha! That was just an excuse to kiss you. I *knew* this would happen. I *knew* he'd make a play for you." She laughed again, as though this new development was *good* news.

What? Frankie wondered. Had all of her friends lost their minds? Aside from the event itself, there was absolutely nothing *good* about Ross kissing her. Furthermore, what on earth would lead her to the assumption that Ross would make a play for her? After a moment, she decided to ask.

April let go a patient sigh. "Frankie, for someone normally so perceptive, there are times when you can be exceedingly thick."

That was twice she'd been told that in the past week, Frankie thought, annoyed. Ross had made the same comment when they'd been discussing Tate and Zora's bet. Ross had thinly accused Zora of plotting their unfortunate trip together, but he had to be wrong. Zora knew they couldn't stand one another. She knew—

Frankie stilled as an inkling of knowledge penetrated her hazy brain. No, she breathed silently. It couldn't be. Zora wouldn't have done this to her. She— She couldn't have.

"It's been obvious to everyone but you that Ross has a thing for you. And before you get all huffy and try to deny it, it's equally obvious that his interest is reciprocated. The melting, steamy kiss we all heard about merely confirms what we've all suspected. You're perfect for each other."

Frankie absorbed April's little bomb until she exploded. Her gaze shot to her door and she belatedly wished she'd closed it. "Have you all lost your *freakin'* minds?" she quietly wailed as every muscle in her body went rigid with alarm. "We're not perfect for each other. We hate each other." Not altogether true, but that was the implied perception.

"No, you don't. The attraction is so hot the rest of us can't stand near you two without feeling the heat. Admit it," she cajoled. "You know it's true."

Zora hadn't paired him up with her to make him miserable—she was matchmaking. Oh, dear God. And Ross had seen it while she had not. Frankie swallowed a groan. Would her mortification never end?

"Admit it," April needled. "I know it's true, and nothing you can say is going to convince me otherwise."

"Fine," Frankie finally relented. "I'll admit to a marginal attraction, but—"

"Ha!"

She squeezed her eyes tightly shut. "But," she continued doggedly, "just because I admit it doesn't mean that it's a good thing. I happen to like greasy foods and the occasional muscle relaxer, too, but that doesn't mean they're good for me."

"Ross is good for you," April replied firmly. "We all know it."

Aside from that being a blatant untruth, Frankie absolutely hated being manipulated in this way. She would decide what was good for her, thank you very much. She would make those decisions, not a bunch of well-meaning meddling friends. "Zora did this on purpose." It was a statement, not a question.

"She had a hunch that the two of you would suit."

Frankie swore hotly. "I'm coming home."

"You can't!" April gasped, evidently realizing just how upset she really was. "Frankie, this has been planned for months."

"Not Ross's part of it, I'll wager." Her eyes narrowed. "Which is precisely what got me into this mess to start with. Their stupid bets."

"Frankie, I know you're upset, but—"

"No, you have no idea." Frankie let go a helpless, tired breath. Frustrated, she paused, tore at a loose thread on the duvet cover. "I'll admit to the attraction, April. I can't deny it and I won't lie. But I— I can't do it. Do you understand? I can't let go, can't give myself to someone that way. It's…" She shrugged abruptly, trying to find the right words. "I, uh… I just can't do it."

April let go a sigh. "Can't or won't?"

"Both."

"Frankie, you're many things—you're ruthless, cool, smart and witty. You're loyal and loving, sweet and tough. But I've never taken you for a coward. What gives?"

"Not me," she said, rubbing her forehead with the palm of her hand. She was exhausted, weary. "Not to that extent."

April made a sad noise. "Oh, Frankie. Won't you even try?" she asked gently. "All men are not your father."

"I know that." And, rationally, she did. But the heart was not always rational, which was why she'd just hang on to it, if it was all the same to everyone. "Look, I need to go. I'll check in with you later."

She disconnected, then curled onto her side and stifled an irritated sob. What had they done? Just what *the hell* had they done?

Dallas

THE CROWD that had greeted them in San Francisco had been a surprise, but Ross found the *mob* that met them in Dallas to be downright frightening.

Frankie had opted to skip dinner the night before, had closed off her part of the bedroom and left him to his own devices. One would think that would have been a good thing—she wouldn't annoy him, he could work, think about the kiss and what a bad idea the kiss had been.

Unfortunately, Ross felt many things, but relief was never one of them. Mostly, though it galled him to admit it, he'd felt...lonely. Knowing that she was in the other room, most likely half-naked, had made him alternately burn and quake.

He'd expected her to blast him for taking advantage of their situation, had expected her to berate his performance as the Duke of Desire. To basically act like her typically surly, provoking self.

The one thing he hadn't expected was for her to hole up in her room and hide from him.

And he knew that was what she was doing. Had she been so unaffected that the incident didn't merit any conversation? Ross wondered. Or, like him, had she been so rattled that she'd just needed some space? Hell, who knew? He certainly didn't, and trying to puzzle out her confounding little mind was like trying to pick up salt one grain at a time—tedious and pointless.

Nevertheless, Frankie was many things, but *quiet* wasn't one of them. She'd pulled back, was regrouping, and he didn't have a single doubt that she'd let him know what she thought. His gaze slid to her delightful rump swinging along in front of him. Sooner or later.

"Looks like Dallas loves *CHiC*," he commented lightly as they made their way up to the front of the room, once again to the tune of "Let's Talk About Sex." Hell, at the rate their crowds were growing, they'd end up needing Atlanta's Turner Field by the time Friday rolled around.

Instead of looking happy, a troubled frown marred the smooth line of her brow.

"What?" he asked, puzzled. "Is this not a good thing?"

"It's good for *CHiC*," she replied grimly. "But not for us."

Ross scowled. That didn't make any sense. "Meaning?"

Frankie slowed as they reached the stage steps, then turned to face him. She pulled in a deep breath, giving him the distinct impression that she'd rehearsed the speech she was gearing up to deliver. Which would explain why he'd gotten the silent treatment on the plane as well, Ross decided.

"I'm only going to say this once, so pay attention. You were right. This whole trip was Zora's idea. She's matchmaking." Frankie bit her lip and looked away. "Apparently, my friends—and I'm assuming Tate as well—think there's some sort of...chemistry between us." She rolled her eyes, but didn't verbally try to deny it. For whatever reason, he found that curiously heartening. "After that little kissing stunt you pulled yesterday, they're convinced of it, and," she sighed, "also, as a result of the kissing stunt, CHiC's e-mail and blog system was inundated with posts citing our amazing, melting tongue-tangling session." Apparently unable to bring herself to meet his gaze, she stared at some fascinating something just over his left shoulder, then huffed a breath. "At any rate, thanks to you," she added pointedly, "I'm sure this crowd is expecting a repeat performance."

Ross felt a grin taunt his lips. "They're expecting me to kiss you again?"

Another exasperated huff slipped out of her supremely carnal mouth. "Didn't you read the signs on the way in?"

"No."

She blinked, stared at him like he was the half-wit she'd called him earlier. "No?"

"No," he repeated. He'd been too busy admiring her ass, but he should probably keep that little tidbit to himself.

She let go another breath. "Yes, Ross, they're expecting you to kiss me again. They're expecting the same heat they *thought* they saw in San Francisco."

Ross sidled a little closer, lowered his voice. "I *thought* there was quite a bit of heat."

She snorted, looked away. "You thought wrong."

He lessened the distance between them again, smiled. "Liar."

She heaved a long-suffering sigh. "Are you always so arrogant?"

"That depends. Are your nipples always hard?"

She inhaled a sharp gasp and cut him a smirking glance. "Is your dick?"

Ross chuckled, not the least bit surprised at her candor and decided to repay it in kind. He hauled her against him, rocked his pelvis forward and swiftly lowered his head, catching her surprised gasp with his mouth. "It is around you, Frankie," he admitted with a resigned laugh. "Always around you." He nudged her forward before she could respond. "Move your ass, dearest. Our fans are waiting."

They wanted heat, Ross thought. Fine, he'd give them some heat. And by the time this session was finished he'd make sure that nothing but ashes remained of the doubts Frankie *pretended* to have about the authenticity of their attraction.

Playtime was over. It was time for truth or consequences.

8

ALWAYS AROUND HER, Frankie thought dimly as she once again gave the floor to Ross. They'd been "on" for the better part of an hour and, just as she'd anticipated, through the power of the Internet, word of their kissing performance had made it with lightning speed to Dallas.

Aside from a few serious questions about birth control and bad lovers, the majority of the questions had been aimed at Ross. Leading ones like, "Could you show us the proper way to French kiss?"—which naturally resulted in another live necking session in which her bones melted and every bit of the reason left in her head went south—and, "What's the most important thing a woman can do to make her man perform better?"

Praise, he'd told the woman succinctly. He'd

likened men to dogs and said that they responded to positive reinforcement better than anything else.

"Good sex equals more sex. We know that. We're not intentionally selfish. Just give us a clue. Howl if you like it. Look," he explained patiently, "men aren't deep enough to be mind readers, particularly when they're diving dick-first into a female. We're thinking one thing, ladies. 'Oh, yeah. I'm gettin' some.'" He laughed. "Then a minute later we're thinking, "Hell, *yeah!* I'm *still* gettin' some.' And when we're done, we're thinking, 'Oh, yeah. I got me some.'" He did a little victory dance, shrugged, then scratched his head self-consciously. A boyish grin pulled at the corner of his too sexy mouth. "Nothing too complicated about that, right?"

Frankie laughed in spite of herself. Ross had moved into his role as the Duke of Desire quite easily. In fact, he'd doled out his opinions in much the same fashion as she did. He was blunt and funny, and if he didn't know the answer, he didn't make up some bullshit line. That was one of Frankie's personal pet peeves. She never pretended to know all the answers. Hell, who could? She valued honesty more, and from the looks of things, so did Ross. Just another facet of his personality she'd be better off not knowing. It only served to make her want him more.

As if that were even possible. The idea that he kept a hard-on around her would absolutely drive her insane. She scoped out his mouth, ass and crotch enough as it was. She damned sure hadn't needed another reason to be pining over his groin.

Frankie checked her watch. Time to wrap things up. "Okay, ladies, we've got time for one more question." She scanned the crowd and randomly picked a person from the sea of hands. "Yes?"

The woman smiled shyly. "My question is for the Duke."

Frankie resisted the urge to roll her eyes. *Big surprise,* she thought resignedly.

"When it comes to oral sex, what's your biggest turn-off?"

Ross looked a bit dumbfounded by that one and a slow smile rolled around his lips. "I didn't realize there were any turn-offs when it came to oral sex," he'd replied. "I always like getting it." A collective laugh moved through the packed room. "But if you'd like some tips on administering it, I'll happily be Frankie's guinea pig." His hand moved to his fly expectantly and he shot her a smile that would have blown the top off a voltage chart. He was incorrigible, Frankie thought, as a reluctant chuckle bubbled up her throat. Odd that she should find that endearing.

She grinned at him. "I think not." She turned back to the woman and quirked a brow. "Did that answer your question?"

"Er…not exactly. What I wanted to know was if there was anything that a *woman* could do to interest a lover in performing that type of…service."

Ah, Frankie thought knowingly. Now they were getting to the crux of the matter. "Well, beyond hygiene—making sure things are neat and clean, so to speak—there's really not. Some men have an aversion to that type of foreplay. Not to *getting* it, as you just heard from Ross, here," she said with a pointed smile in his direction. "But *giving* it. And—" Frankie laughed "—if I wasn't getting it, I damn sure wouldn't be giving it, if you get my drift. What's good for the goose is good for the gander."

"She's right," Ross seconded, much to her surprise. "There needs to be equality in the bedroom, a balance. Both partners need to give it all they've got, otherwise the sex is merely mediocre. Granted, mediocre sex is better than no sex," he qualified jokingly, "but why anyone would settle for less than the best is beyond me."

"So are you saying you give it one hundred percent every time?" someone called out.

Another lazy grin rolled around his lips and he cut those incredibly sexy eyes to her. She drowned in a sea of brown, blue and green flecks. "Every time."

Frankie let go a small breath and her belly did a little roll. A taunt? she wondered. Or a promise? Either way the message remained the same. *Great sex. Every time.*

Sounded like a good note to end on, she decided abruptly. She thanked everyone for coming, reminded them to be sure and keep visiting the Web site, then she and Ross, who'd balked at wearing the shirt today, citing a lasagna stain he'd—deliberately, she imagined—gotten on it last night—made their escape out a side door and into a service elevator. These, she'd learned halfway through their talk, weren't your everyday average women—the majority of them were romance writers and make-up gurus who happened to be hosting simultaneous conferences at the hotel.

Frankie would love a facial, and the idea of curling up with a good book and forgetting all this crap with Ross was incredibly tempting, but unfortunately she didn't have the time. They were scheduled for an early flight into Chicago in the morning.

Given the crowded accommodations, they'd be better off ordering room service than trying to get a table in, or even near, the hotel. Which, considering the predatory way some of those women were looking at Ross, Frankie imagined would be for the best. She had enough to contend with—i.e. the near-nuclear attraction brewing between them—to worry about possibly ending up in a jealous brawl over Ross. Was he *her* Duke of Desire? No. But he was *CHiC*'s Duke of Desire and she had an obligation to make sure that he didn't do anything stupid—

or anything that would piss her off, and force her to make a fool of herself—while he was on staff.

In all fairness, she really wasn't worried about Ross doing anything stupid—of the two of them, she was the most likely candidate to lose her temper and act foolish. Frankie had a short fuse and several courses of anger management hadn't done a damned thing to help control her hot-headed Italian temper. She grinned. It was better than keeping things bottled up, allowing them to fester, she supposed, but times like now, when her emotions were running so close to the surface, she really wished she had a better handle on things.

Her father had always used her temper against her, made her feel weak for not being able to control it. She knew now that it had simply been a way for him to goad her—he'd been very proficient at finding ways to make her wretched—and that if it hadn't been that, he would have simply found something else. Still…

"Well?" Ross asked. "How do you think that went?"

Frankie nodded. "Good." Remembering his

comment about positive reinforcement, she decided his efforts deserved a small crumb of praise. "You're doing quite well."

He blinked and pretended to be overwhelmed by the compliment. "Quite well," he repeated with an exaggerated show of enthusiasm. "Wow." He dabbed at his crinkled eyes. "I, uh… I think I might cry."

Frankie bit the inside of her cheek to keep from laughing. "Asshole."

Ross chuckled. "So where are we going tomorrow, what time do we leave, and when will we get there?"

"We're going to Chicago, we'll need to leave around six, and we'll reach the hotel about ten."

He nodded, seemingly taking it all in. "So what are our plans for the rest of the night, boss?"

Frankie staunchly ignored the hint of innuendo lurking beneath the surface of his voice. "Room service, for sure." They'd missed lunch, so she was starving. "Then you'll probably want to work on—" She frowned and arched an eyebrow. "What exactly are you working on, again?"

"The Maxwell account," Ross replied. "It would bore you. It's not nearly as exciting as talking about sex all day. In fact, I've decided I prefer your job."

The elevator delivered them to their floor. "Yeah, well, don't get too comfortable, Duke," she told him. "This is a one-woman gig and it's mine."

Frankie fished the keycard from her purse and planted it into the lock. She vaguely recalled hearing the desk clerk mention another suite, but they hadn't had time to come up and scope out their rooms. Their connecting flight had been delayed, which had barely left them time to hit a bathroom before making their session, much less come upstairs. Their luggage had gone one way and they had gone another.

Frankie pushed open the door, and the single bed and sitting room zoomed too swiftly into view, making her belly alternately inflate and deflate with a rapidity that left her a bit breathless.

One bed. One room. No way to escape. *One hundred percent. Every time.*

Oh, shit.

Ross sidled in around her and it took him even less time to discern what had been immediately obvious to her. "Looks like Zora's upping the ante, eh?"

Frankie swallowed as a vision of she and Ross vibrating the bed across the room materialized in the private theater of her mind. She let go a shaky breath. "Yeah," she conceded with a grunt of irritation. "It does."

Though it would have been so easy for him to make a glib comment, or to take the opportunity to make an advance, Ross did the last thing she expected—he offered to ask for another room.

"I don't mind," he told her, those compelling eyes warm with something she could only conclude was respect. A novel experience, that, Frankie thought, touched beyond reason. Geez, every time she turned around Ross was doing something like this. Forcing her to revise her opinions, making her like him. She couldn't afford to like him, dammit. Lust? Sure. Like? No way. Like could too easily make way for an even more devastating emotion.

Ross rubbed a hand over the back of his neck.

"Look, Frankie, I'm not gonna lie to you. After the last couple of days, it's obvious that I'm attracted to you—have been since the first moment I saw you—and I..." A crooked smile claimed his lips, momentarily at a loss for words. "Well, I think I've given you some pretty irrefutable proof of that." He glanced significantly below his waist.

She inclined her head, chewed the corner of her lip. Yeah, that was certainly the truth. That mouthwatering hard-on she'd felt rock against her belly this afternoon had all but made her come on the spot.

He let go a small pent-up breath. "But I'm not into seducing women who don't want to be seduced—it's not my thing—so just know that this is going to play out the way you want it to." His lips formed another half grin. "Just... Just say the word and I'm on the couch in the lobby."

The coward in her, the one who questioned her own self-control thought sending Ross to the couch would be a wise idea, but the rational part knew that punishing him for Zora's meddling didn't seem particularly fair. The fact that she was even thinking about *fair* and *Ross* in the same sentence told her that she needed to take a serious reality check. But in the end, she just couldn't justify making him that uncomfortable when he'd ended up being, of all things, an ally.

She couldn't tell him that though, so instead opted for her old friend, sarcasm. "Don't be ridiculous. You're not *that* irresistible."

Recognizing the ploy for what it was, Ross chuckled softly. "Gotta put me in my place, don't you?"

"Yeah. The floor, slick. I'm not sharing a bed." She moved deeper into the room, dropped her purse onto the low-slung dresser.

He laughed again, a sexy rumble that licked her nerve endings and sent sparklers of heat fizzing through her body. "I'm more irresistible than you want to admit, otherwise you wouldn't be worried about having my *resistible* ass in that king-sized bed with you."

Now that was a little too perceptive for comfort. "Fine," Frankie returned, immediately wishing she could cut her tongue out. "You can sleep in the bed. Just make sure you stay on your side and keep your hands to yourself."

He cocked his head. "I will if you will."

She couldn't think of a fitting comeback, so she merely rolled her eyes and tried to impart her complete disgust with his continued arrogance. At least, this is what she hoped she managed to imply, because what she'd really been thinking was more along the lines of *damn, damn, damn, damn—I'm doomed.*

Doomed, doomed, doomed.

ROSS WATCHED Frankie sidle away and had to forcibly quell the urge to tackle her. He didn't know why he felt this sudden urge to subdue her, to put her in her place—knees or back? Knees or back? he wondered—but the desire was there all the same. He wanted to wrestle her down, nuzzle her neck, then play a little bed sport that would leave them both satisfied and sweaty, limp and laughing.

Nevertheless, he'd put the ball firmly into her court and he intended for it to stay there until she was ready to lob it back at him. He'd meant what he'd told her. He didn't have to seduce unwilling lovers, and he damned sure wasn't going to start with her. When she wanted him—not if, there was no doubt about that—then she possessed the experience to let him know.

Of course that didn't mean he wasn't above pressing an advantage. He didn't necessarily appreciate Zora's methods but he damned sure wasn't going to miss an opportunity to make the most of them.

Ross tugged his shirt free of his waistband, drew it over his head and tossed it over the arm of a nearby chair.

Frankie stilled. Moistened her lips. "What are you doing?"

"Getting comfortable. It's hotter than hell in here, don't you think?"

She crossed her arms over her chest and regarded him with amusement. "If you're thinking the sight of your bare chest is going to make me go wild with lust, you'd better think again." She let go a sigh. "Honestly, Ross, I'd have thought you'd come up with something a little more original."

Original or not, she seemed suddenly mesmerized by the pattern of hair on his chest. Gratified, Ross pushed a hand through his hair, collapsed onto the end of the bed and fell back.

He stared at the ceiling. "Ah," he sighed. "That's much better. Cooler."

He covertly cracked one eye open and noticed that Frankie didn't look cool at all—in fact, she looked distinctly hot. Her cheeks had reddened—surely to God he hadn't made her blush, Ross thought, astounded—and her breathing seemed to be a smidge on the labored side.

"Whatever," she finally replied. "Just keep your pants on."

Ross rolled over and snagged the remote from the night stand, idly channel surfed while Frankie pretended to be looking at everything in the room but him. "Since we're staying in tonight, why don't we catch a movie?"

Silence, then, "What kind of movie?" she asked warily.

A short burst of laughter erupted from his throat as what she was thinking suddenly surfaced in the quagmire of his mind. "Not porn, I can assure you." Ross grunted. "Watching other people get it on is *not* what cranks my tractor." And it wasn't. He'd just as soon watch paint dry. Who'd want to watch sex as opposed to having it? "I prefer comedies," he told her, "but if you'd like to watch a legal thriller or a horror movie, that's fine. Just be prepared to hold my hand," he teased. "I scare easily."

Frankie's lips twitched and those dark brown eyes glinted with reluctant humor. "You're not afraid of anything, you great jackass. You're too damned full of yourself."

"Ah, see, that's an improvement. You used to think I was only full of shit."

This time she did laugh, a delighted chuckle that bubbled freely up her throat. It was a wonderful sound, Ross decided, one he'd love to hear again.

His phone vibrated at his waist, interrupting the comfortable silence which had fallen between them. He winced, afraid to even look at the display.

Amy had called repeatedly over the past two days, seemingly in a near panic because she couldn't run him to ground. She'd filled his voice mail and, according to Charley, had been by his house several times. With a resigned sigh, Ross finally snagged his cell from the clip and checked the caller ID. *Charley.* Relief loosened every dread-locked muscle as he answered the call.

"Hey," Ross said. A careful peek at Frankie confirmed that she wasn't even trying not to eavesdrop on his conversation. She was openly staring at him and the smile she'd worn a moment ago had once again slipped back into a woefully familiar smirk. She caught his gaze, heaved a disgusted breath and shook her head. Ross frowned. What was that all about? he wondered.

"Ross?"

"Yeah, Charley," he said, turning his attention back to the call. "What's up? Otis all right?"

"Yeah, Otis is fine. Look, I know you're busy and I hate to bother you…but that Amy woman isn't going away."

Ross squeezed his eyes shut and swore.

"She's calling a few times every hour, sometimes more, and when I checked your mail yesterday, there were several letters in there from her. She's…" Charley paused, more than likely trying to think of a PC way of saying that she was crazy. "Look, Ross, this chick has got a problem. I think you need a restraining order. She sat out in your driveway last night until after midnight, and she probably wouldn't have left then, but Mom came over and threatened to call the police. What do you want me to do?"

Ross rested his elbow against his knee and rubbed the bridge of his nose, trying to come up with some semblance of a plan. Though he didn't want to admit it, things were escalating. Rapidly. When he got back he would definitely have to go the professional help route and see about getting a restraining order. There was simply no other choice. He'd tried everything else. Clearly, she wasn't going to respond to his repeated attempts to break things off.

Shit.

Shit, shit, shit.

It was just so damned embarrassing. His gaze slid to Frankie, who'd at least begun to pretend like she wasn't listening. His lips twisted. He could just imagine her reaction to his stalker news. Hell, she already thought his head was too big for his shoulders. She'd undoubtedly have a field day with it. He was so good at predicting her reactions that it took very little effort to imagine the look on her face, hear the condescension and humor in her voice. *So, you really do think you're irresistible, eh, Ross?*

He muttered another hot oath. "Are you uncomfortable staying there?" Ross finally asked him. "Would you rather take Otis and go home?"

"No!" Charley immediately replied. Apparently being the inadvertent victim of a stalker was preferable to staying at home with his mother, Ross thought with a faint smile. "I just thought you should know, that's all," Charley explained.

"Right." Ross stared at the floor, searched his mind for the right kind of advice, then realized he didn't have it to offer. "Look, just keep doing what you're doing," he finally told him. "Let the machine pick up, unless it's me. Don't go to the door, unless it's your mother. I'll, uh, take care of it when I get home, and if you think you'd be better off at your own house, then I'll understand. Just keep me posted on what's happening, okay?"

"Sure."

"Thanks, buddy," Ross told him. "Take care of my dog."

Frankie pounced the instant he disconnected. She shot him a falsely sweet smile. "Problem?" she asked.

"Nah," Ross replied with an unconcerned shake of his head. Tension camped in the back of his neck. This was one conversation he *wasn't* going to have with her. She'd make fun and belittle, and dammit, there was absolutely nothing funny about having a woman harass the living hell out of you.

"Sounds like a problem," she pressed infuriatingly. "Your house/dog sitter can't answer your phone or go to your door. What?" she asked with a thoughtful cock of her gorgeous head, an infuriating smiled shaping her provokingly carnal mouth. "Is it a pissed-off papa, or a thwarted ex?"

"It's nothing," Ross insisted tightly, purposely avoiding her gaze.

Frankie stilled, seemed to fully consider him. He could feel the weight of that heavy stare, could literally feel her probing for a way to slip inside his head. "I'm sorry," she finally said, and she sounded truly repentant. "It's none of my business."

Hands laced behind his head, Ross sent her a careful look. Frankie's expression had lost its seemingly perpetual smirk and a mask of genuine concern and curiosity had taken its place. She'd toed her shoes off, sat down in one of the wing chairs and tucked her feet underneath her body. Her hair tumbled sleekly over her shoulders, the blue-black locks particularly striking against that creamy-olive complexion.

She wore a linen pantsuit a shade darker than a ripe cantaloupe, and the picture she made in that instant was at once relaxed and sexy. Approachable. There was something slightly different about her, Ross realized, and an instant later a prick of understanding broke though the cloudy confines of his mind—the guard had come down.

Or at least partially.

Once again the urge to spill his guts, to confide in her hit him, and this time harder than the last. It would be so easy to share it with the person she presented right now, to spew it all out— the irritation, frustration and anger—and have her offer outrage and *tsk*s of understanding on his behalf.

So easy…and yet too hard. He winced, let go a breath. It was just too damned embarrassing. Too hard to admit. A stalker, for pity's sake,

Ross thought, disgusted. It was degrading. Emasculating. But most of all, ridiculous.

"Toss me that room service menu, would you?" he asked her, trying vainly to sound normal, to pretend like the awkward moment never happened. "I'm hungry."

Time to practice a little Southern psychology, Ross decided.

When in doubt, eat.

9

Chicago

FRANKIE COVERED her mouth to hide a yawn, waited patiently outside one of the trendy boutiques located on Chicago's historic Magnificent Mile. She had no idea what Ross was doing in there. He'd spotted something of interest, though, and left her standing outside while he'd hurried in, presumably to make a purchase.

She leaned against a brightly painted cow and waited for him, enjoying the crisp smell of autumn, the slight rustle of fallen leaves whirling along the sidewalk. When a couple of bickering squirrels could no longer hold her interest, she turned to people-watching, then ultimately to the one thing that she'd been trying to avoid thinking about.

This morning.

She'd woken up in the exact position she'd feared she'd end up in last night when she'd crawled beneath the covers with him—a hard body at her back, not to mention a hard-*on* riding high enough on her rump to make her alternately wiggle and squirm—and a warm hand snugged loosely against her muddled belly.

Mama mia.

The mere memory made her palms tingle and a languid, winding heat twine through her limbs and take root in her womb. Resisting him was becoming increasingly harder and if he didn't do something stupid soon to ruin this good-guy perception, she'd undoubtedly end up being the one who did something ignorant.

Like letting him back in her bed, only without the pretense of sleep.

True to his word, other than shamelessly losing articles of his clothing so that she could better admire just exactly what she was missing, Ross had left the ball in her court and hadn't tried to steal it back from her. They'd ordered room service, settled in and watched a movie, then chatted for a while, and eventually—and

not as awkwardly as she would have thought—
went to bed. It had been quite…cozy.

Though she'd wanted to press him further
about the bizarre conversation she'd overheard,
Frankie had ultimately decided against it. She
could tell Ross was truly troubled about whatever it was, and she knew from experience that
there were some things that were simply too
private. He'd guarded his responses to Charley
very carefully, but she'd gleaned enough from
his side of it to realize that something was disturbingly wrong.

Though she knew it was unreasonable, it sort
of pricked that he didn't trust her enough to confide in her, but given the hostile way they normally communicated, she couldn't very well
blame him for holding back. It was funny, though,
Frankie thought, her gaze turning inward. For a
moment there, she'd thought he was going to.

At any rate, it was probably for the best that
he hadn't. She was having a hard enough time
keeping her wits about her as it was—and more
importantly, keeping her hands to herself. The
last thing she needed was to deepen their already strengthening…friendship.

Frankie paused, letting the idea sink in. The term was a little too intimate for her liking, but she had to admit that it fit. At some point over the past three days Ross had gone from being a guy she was devastatingly attracted to on a physical level, to one who'd engaged her mentally— cerebrally—as well. That bizarre familiarity she'd felt when she'd first met him had resumed full force and she knew that she was in serious danger of slipping over the edge, of losing herself in him.

Of, God forbid, trusting him.

For reasons beyond her immediate understanding, there was something about Ross that begged her to believe in honorable men and happily-ever-after. She'd listened to him dole out advice, share his theories on everything from dating to sex and had been surprised to find that their views jived with startling precision.

He wasn't opposed to telling a little white lie on harmless issues, but was brutally frank when it came to what he expected out of a relationship. Or more accurately, what a woman *shouldn't* expect out of him in a relationship.

Too many men would tell a girl anything to

lure her into bed, then the balls they'd been so eager to show off suddenly shriveled up and headed for higher ground when it came to something as courteous as a phone call. That had been a startling accurate insight, Frankie had thought, one that she'd been grudgingly impressed by.

Other than his blatant attempt to pretend to like that hideous shirt she'd made him wear, he'd been unfailingly honest with her. About everything, including the fact that he was attracted to her and *had* been attracted to her from the very beginning.

Frankie generally repaid truths in kind, but for some reason admitting to Ross—any more than her rebellious nipples already had—that she wanted him, too, was something she was having a hard time getting past her lips. He knew, though, the scheming wretch.

Last night he'd waltzed out of the bathroom with a towel wrapped precariously low on his lean hips, his skin dewy and damp, his dark golden hair curling wet and loosely about his face, and she'd felt a hot zing pulse between her legs, then hit her nipples, and her mouth had actually watered. She'd pictured herself walking up behind him, slipping her arms around his waist and gently nipping his shoulder with her teeth. The vision had been so real, she'd actually caught herself walking toward him before she realized that she'd gotten out of her chair.

This sort of attraction—the intensity of her feelings—went well beyond the scope of her understanding. She wanted him more than she'd ever wanted anything in her life, felt like she couldn't breathe if he didn't kiss her again, and whereas she used to somewhat dread performing on demand in front of a roomful of people, Frankie had found herself eagerly anticipating each new session because it meant that she'd get to taste him again, to feel the hard thrilling length of his body pressed tightly against hers.

This morning's session had rounded out with them in another spine-tingling lip lock and, rather than keeping things PG-13, Ross had covertly—oh-so-wonderfully—copped a feel. By the end of the week, she'd be so miserably horny that she wouldn't care if he backed her against the podium and took her there in front of a roomful of people. She knew some people were into making it in public places, but that had never been one of her fantasies.

In her sex-with-Ross dreams, they were usually in her bed—which was odd in and of itself because Frankie had never brought a man home with her, much less allowed one into her private sanctuary. The fact that her subconscious would let Ross into her room wasn't lost on her. Some part of her trusted him whether she wanted to or not.

Ross chose that minute to walk out of the store. He wore a white button-down shirt open at the throat and cuffed at the wrists, and a pair of worn jeans that molded to him in all the right places. They hugged his crotch particularly well, a fact that made her belly clench and her toes curl.

With an endearing smile that could only be deemed nervous, Ross held the bag out to her. The wind ruffled his hair and those old-soul eyes glinted with an emotion she couldn't readily discern. "This is for you."

Frankie's eyes widened and her heart skipped a beat. "What?"

"This is for you," he repeated, gesturing to the

bag. "Go on," he told her, smiling crookedly. "Take it."

Other than the sporadic box of chocolates on Valentine's Day, Frankie wasn't accustomed to getting gifts. Like the tooth fairy, Christmas had ended at her house when she was old enough to know that Santa Claus didn't exist. In addition to being a bully, her father had also been cheap. Of course, in his defense he'd needed every extra penny to keep up his mistresses. Another uncharitable thought, but the truth all the same.

Shaken, Frankie didn't know what to say, what to do, and had to dredge the remnants of her brain to remember to mutter a somewhat thready thank-you. She finally accepted the bag and, with the breath lodged firmly in her lungs, opened it up and peeked inside.

"Oh," she gasped, losing the air she'd been holding. "Oh, Ross." A stained-glass window-catcher of a multicolored hummingbird lay nestled in a pillow of tissue paper. It was gorgeous, unlike anything she'd ever seen. Heart racing, mouth dry, she looked up questioningly at him. "Why did—"

He lifted a shoulder in a negligent shrug, then

bent down and placed a lingering kiss on the tip of her nose. "It reminded me of you," he said simply. She felt his gaze trace the lines of her face, linger on her mouth. "Fragile, but strong."

Frankie's throat tightened and the backs of her eyelids stung. She dragged in a shaky breath. That had to be *the best* compliment she'd ever been given.

"Thanks, Ross," she said softly, unable to come up with anything more substantial at the moment. A bubble of air expanded in her chest. "It's—" She cleared her throat. "It's lovely."

He slung an affectionate arm around her shoulders and propelled her forward. "Then it suits you, doesn't it?"

The swaddling haze of unexpected pleasure lasted right up until they walked back into the hotel. The last person Frankie expected to see standing at the bank of elevators was her father and his latest *friend*. The last time she'd seen him, he'd been nibbling a bagel—from the Bagel Girl's breast. Frankie had walked out of the family business then and had never looked back. Years of hurt, anger and frustration welled up inside her, forcing a breath of utter disgust out of her mouth and she drew up short.

Apparently sensing the abrupt change in her mood, Ross stilled beside her. "Frankie?"

No doubt her mother was at home, standing by a window, waiting for his worthless, cheating ass to come home, Frankie thought bitterly. Her mouth soured with the metallic taste of anger.

Ross followed her gaze, then looked back at her, a perplexed line furrowing his brow. "What's wrong?"

Frankie didn't purposely ignore him, but the short fuse which determined the length of her patience had already started to burn. Without thinking, she marched forward until her father finally caught sight of her. He smiled, but the warmth didn't match the chill in his cold, dark eyes. "What a surprise, Frank," he murmured smoothly, drawing the short, blond woman at his side a little closer. "I didn't expect to see you here."

Ross moved in behind her and for whatever reason, the fact that he had her back made her feel a bit stronger, a bit braver. "I'm sure you didn't," she returned just as coolly. "Just out of curiosity, does your wife know where you are?"

Frankie purposely lingered over the term *wife,* but the blonde didn't so much as betray a blink, meaning she knew perfectly well that she man she was with was married. And she didn't care. What was wrong with people? Frankie wondered, resisting the pressing urge to scream. Was there no respect left for the sanctity of marriage? None at all?

A flash of anger lit her father's gaze. "She does," he answered.

Frankie smiled sweetly. "Then the better question would be, does she know you're not alone?"

"That's really none of your business," he replied with an infuriating little laugh. "I see a year touting sexual cures hasn't improved your disposition a bit. Perhaps you'd be better served to find a new vocation, eh, Frank?" His gaze slid to Ross, seemed to take his measure and find him lacking. "Or a new lover. This one clearly hasn't managed to bridle you yet. But then it's been my experience that whores are generally harder to take to the bit."

Ross came around her so quickly he knocked her off balance. He grabbed her father by the throat and shoved him against the wall. The blonde who'd been attached to her father's arm squealed and jumped out of the way.

"Look, Jack," Ross said threateningly, his face an angry thundercloud of white-hot fury. "I don't know who the hell you are, but you'd bet ter apologize to the lady *right now—*" he banged the older man's head against the wall a couple of times for emphasis "—or there's going to be hell to pay. Am I making myself clear?"

Stupidly, her father didn't seem the least bit intimidated. He merely laughed. "A lady, huh? Bet you love that, don't you, Junior?"

"I'm going to count to three," Ross threatened through gritted teeth. "Then I'm going to make your dentist real happy."

"Awful lot of trouble for a piece, isn't it, friend?"

Ross snapped. His fist came back, then landed a solid blow into her father's jaw. She heard the sickening crunch of breaking bone and, with a gratifying *oomph* of pain, he crum-pled like a ragdoll and fell to the floor. With an-other squeal of fright, the blonde hurried to him. "Frank, oh, Frank!"

Ross shook his hand, turned around, grabbed her arm and propelled her away from the scene. Hotel security was swiftly bearing toward them. "Who the hell was that?" he demanded angrily.

"Congratulations," Frankie said hollowly. "You just met my father."

ASTOUNDED, Ross's eyes threatened to come out of their sockets. He drew up short, felt his jaw drop. "Your father?" That sorry SOB who had just called Frankie a whore was *her father*?

"The one and only," she told him, her voice curiously flat. "A delightful fellow, isn't he?"

Ross jabbed an elevator call button, shoved his aching hand through his hair. He didn't know what to say. Granted his own parents hadn't been the greatest, but this… This went well beyond anything he could have imagined.

Then something else clicked into place. He'd kept calling her Frank, or more tellingly, *Junior*—not Frankie. *Trust me. You aren't the only person who mistook me for a boy when I was that age.* That bastard, Ross thought, his eyes narrowing as he made the connection. Her father had given her that terrible haircut, not her mother as he'd originally concluded.

With a gentle hand at the small of her back, he guided her into the elevator. "What's your name?"

"You know my name."

"No," Ross said impatiently as he stabbed the correct number for their floor. "Your *given* name."

"Francesca Grace." Looking curiously unreadable, she shot him a half smile. "Put it together that quickly, did you?"

Ross scowled. "He's a bastard."

"That he is…and I'm the reminder of the son he never had."

Every muscle in Ross's body vibrated with anger. He set his teeth so hard he feared they'd crack. "I don't care what you are, that's no excuse for what he called you."

"You mean whore?" Frankie eyes rounded significantly and she laughed without humor. "That was nothing. Believe me, he's called me much worse. And my mother worse than that."

Her voice was flat, absent of emotion, and those extraordinary eyes, the ones that had glittered with unexpected joy just moments ago when he'd given her the hummingbird were curiously lacking any feeling right now as well.

God, that had been particularly heartbreaking. Ross had seen the stained glass in the window, the image of the hummingbird—the seamless blend of fragility and strength—and had known that it was perfect for Frankie. He saw those same qualities in her. Ordinarily he didn't buy gifts for other people, but something about that imagery had clicked for him, and nothing short of getting it for her would do.

Then he'd handed it to her, and the sheer look of delight on her face—the realization that she didn't often receive gifts—had made him feel like…a better man, Ross decided. His chest had expanded with so much air it had been a miracle he hadn't floated right off the ground.

She did that to him. Made him feel like he could conquer the world, or at the very least, leap over a small building, he thought wryly.

As for the scene downstairs, decking her father had been pure instinct. He'd insulted her, ergo he had to apologize or suffer the consequences.

That was the way it worked in the World According to Ross.

Her father had *wrongly* chosen not to apologize, so Ross had been left with no choice but to give him the default prize—a right hook to his weak, smart-assed jaw.

He slid a considering look at Frankie, tensely waited for the elevator to deliver them to their floor. Though it had felt right—hell, good even—at the time, now he wasn't so certain he'd made the right decision. Since it had been obvious that she'd known him, in hindsight Ross wondered if maybe he should have asked who the guy was before he pummeled the hell out of him.

He let go a resigned breath. In any case it was too late now. He'd already hit him and, knowing what he knew now, Ross was of the opinion that somebody should have decked the bastard years ago.

Repeatedly.

They finally reached their floor. Without so much as a single word or a backward glance, Frankie exited the elevator and started down the hall. He wasn't accustomed to her silence and frankly, the fact that she was so quiet now made his gut knot with dread.

He knew she had a short fuse—her temper was legendary and he'd just seen a good first-hand account of that fact downstairs. Was she so pissed off that she couldn't speak? Ross wondered. Had he made her so mad that she couldn't manage to unhinge her jaw long enough to blast him?

Hell, he didn't know, but this continued silence was absolutely wrecking his nerves. If she was pissed off at him for hitting her father, then why didn't she just tell him? What? he wondered. Was he too close to the eye of the storm?

Unable to stand the silence any longer, Ross opened the door to their room—another shared one, bless Zora's twisted, scheming little heart—then followed her inside. He let go a heavy breath. "Look, Frankie—"

Cool as you please—to his slack-jawed astonishment—she set her bag aside and began to unbutton her shirt. That dark-as-sin gaze tangled with his, and one of the most beautiful smiles he'd ever seen—gorgeous because it infected every available form of expression in her face— slid across her lips. "I've still got the ball, right?"

Ross developed a temporary speech impediment at the sight of her plump cleavage spilling over the cups of her bra. "You do," he finally croaked.

She shrugged unhurriedly out of her shirt, let it fall to the floor. Her zipper sang as she slid it down, then, looking like a wet-dream fantasy come to life, she painstakingly slipped her pants down over her sweetly curved hips and kicked them aside. She wore matching undies, a black lacy bra and high-cut equally lacy panties.

The equivalent of a nice bow on a better present.

"Get naked, slick," she said. "Because I'm about to score."

Then, laughing delightedly, she launched herself at him.

10

SHE WAS DOOMED, Frankie decided fatalistically as she walked into their room. Heart hammering, hands shaking, she set her purse and bag aside, then turned to face Ross and began to slide the buttons free from their closures down the front of her shirt.

Ross's eyes zoomed in on the bare skin she was revealing every second and a half and he went preternaturally still.

Frankie smoothly shrugged out of her shirt and let it land on the floor. Her hands moved to the snap at her waist, then her zipper.

Well, that had been the last damned straw, she thought, resigning herself to a melting orgasm and a broken heart. The gift had nearly sent her over the edge, but what Ross had just done for her downstairs—planting that magnificent right hook into her father's arrogant, cruel jaw—the one thing that she'd *always* wanted to do, but had never had the nerve, much less the strength to try... Now that was something special.

She'd never had a champion.

Ever.

Frankie's throat clogged with emotion and something warm and light moved into her chest. Even her mother had very rarely come to her defense. That Ross had listened to one ugly comment, then reacted without the slightest bit of hesitation on her behalf spoke volumes about how he felt about her. About the kind of man he was.

Oh, Frankie didn't have any illusions about him falling in love with her—though she grimly suspected she'd just flipped head over heels for him—she knew better than to expect a profession of undying love once this week was over. Knew better than to expect that she'd be anything more than another notch on his bedpost. She let go a shaky breath. But if nothing else, Ross Hartford respected her, and for now—and probably forever, though she flatly refused to think about it—that would simply have to do.

Tonight she'd tell herself that her heart wouldn't get broken.

Tonight she'd tell herself that he was probably in love with her, too.

Tonight she'd believe in happy endings and honorable men.

Tonight she'd believe in Ross.

Frankie slipped her hands down over her hips, simultaneously sending the pants down her legs, then kicked them aside. Anticipation sent her pulse rocketing through her veins and the mere knowledge of what she was about to do—what she was about to get—made her breasts tingle and her panties moist.

The combination of finally having him—and the happy realization that her father was somewhere in this hotel with a broken jaw—pushed a giddy laugh up her throat and, instead of dragging out the tension by sauntering toward him—her original plan—she hurled herself at him, causing him to grunt and stagger backward into the door.

Graceless, yes, Frankie thought dimly as Ross's hot hands caught her naked back...but effective.

Besides, containing herself on their excruci-atingly long ride up to their room had been hard enough. It had taken every iota of willpower she possessed to keep from launching herself at him in the elevator.

But she hadn't.

She'd absorbed the absolute joy of the mo-ment and savored the idea that she was finally going to have him. Months and months of mis-erable, unrelieved sexual frustration were about to come to an end, and for that she wanted a bed.

They could try the elevator later.

Ross growled low in his throat, nuzzled her neck, sending a wave of gooseflesh racing across her belly.

Much later, she amended, her breath catching in her throat.

Truth for truth time, Frankie thought. She licked a path up the side of his neck, tasted the musky scent of his shower gel and the faintest hint of autumn air. Mmm. Delicious. "I have a confession to make."

Ross expertly unsnapped her bra, sending her breasts tumbling against his chest. "I'm...listening."

No, he wasn't. He was staring at her and she liked it. "I've wanted you for a long time."

Ross drew back and those slumberous kaleidoscope eyes twinkled with the merest flash of male satisfaction. He backed her up and started deliberately maneuvering her toward the bed. "How long?" he asked, his voice low and husky.

"Since the first time I saw you." The back of her legs hit the mattress and she sank onto the edge of the bed. A thrill of excitement moved through her.

Ross's fingers jumped from button to button with swift efficiency as he quickly divested himself of his own shirt. *Taut muscle, flat masculine nipples, an inverted triangle of crisp golden hair...*

He shook his head and affected a disappointed sigh. "We're not even gonna talk about how much time we've wasted."

Frankie leaned back on her elbows, watched him fish his wallet from his back pocket. "I wasn't ready," she explained, compelled for some reason to let him know.

Ross deliberately plucked a couple of condoms from his wallet, tossed them onto the bed, then kicked his pants and briefs aside, revealing every tantalizing—incredibly long—inch of his body for her bold perusal. "And you are now?"

Oh, God, yes, she thought, and even if she wasn't, now wasn't the time to be asking. How could she say no to *that?*

Frankie nodded, scooted back onto the bed where he could comfortably join her. "I am."

Ross stalked like a panther up the length of her body, licked the inside of her thigh, then playfully tugged her drenched panties off with his teeth. Frankie's stomach fluttered and her feminine muscles clenched, coating her folds with another rush of liquid heat. A second later that talented tongue swirled around her belly button, and then landed deliciously over her nipple. "Then I think we should practice a little time management."

Frankie let go a shuddering breath, slid her hands up and over the supple muscle of his back and sides. Hard and soft, warm and...*hers.* If by that he meant that he'd take her hard and fast now, and save a slow session for later, then they were most definitely in complete agreement.

A part of her wanted to sink and savor—sink

beneath the sensation of his touch, savor every orgasmic vibration he could pull from her body. But another part, the desperate, mindless, *Please, God, now!* part couldn't stand the idea of waiting another second. She'd wanted him for too long, needed him too desperately.

"I'm for time management," she said, her voice slightly husky to her own ears. She pulled his head down for a kiss, feasted on his mouth until she was drunk with the taste of him. "If it'll get you inside me faster." She sucked his tongue into her mouth, felt him quiver above her. "One hundred percent of you," she murmured significantly, remembering that taunting promise he'd made about giving one hundred percent every time. She rocked her pelvis up, purposely putting his shaft against her aching, weepy folds.

Ross chuckled darkly, the sound at once sexy and compelling. He bent and pulled the crown of her breast deep into his mouth, pushed against her, expertly bumping her clit. "Oh, b-babe," he stuttered, a look of intense pleasure on his face. "You're going to be the death of me."

"Yeah, well, it's bad form to kick off before I come, so try to hang around for a little while."

He drew back and bit the side of his lip, his smile endearingly crooked. "I'll do my damnedest."

"That's all I can ask," she deadpanned. "After all, you're not a mind reader."

"Are you always this chatty during sex?"

She pulled a thoughtful frown. "I dunno. Are we having it yet?"

"Is that your way of telling me to hurry up?"

"Ah," she sighed delightedly. "So you *are* a mind reader."

Ross chuckled again, reached across her and snagged a condom, then swiftly rolled it into place. When he would have moved between her legs, Frankie rolled him over and straddled him, felt the hot length of him bump against her pulsing folds. The contact pushed the breath from her lungs, made her quiver deep in her womb.

She couldn't wait another second, tilted her hips until she felt him nudge her channel, then slowly—deliberately—impaled herself on him. Her lids fluttered shut and her head suddenly felt too heavy for her neck. She seated herself firmly, took every last magnificent inch, then clenched her muscles around him and rocked back and forth once. "Game," she said brokenly.

Ross's lips peeled away from his teeth and he set his hands on her hips, gently increasing the pressure. She rocked again, impossibly could feel her body quickening, racing toward release... "Set."

Oh, mercy. She felt the first flash of beginning climax, could feel her sex ripening, readying for release. Anticipating the break, slid up and down, then she clamped hard, pulling him deeper. Predictably, it hit. Lights danced behind her closed lids and she bowed from the shock of sensation.

"Match," she cried as the orgasm crested and broke though her, pulling her under, lifting her up, delivering her from months, years, eons of sexual frustration. She flew apart, then reassembled and, when the last tremor of release pulsed through her she knew that she was different. One of her parts was missing, a significant one located beneath her ribs, up and to the left—her heart.

She was unquestionably, undoubtedly, undeniably head over heels in love with Ross Hartford.

"YOU THINK this is what Zora had in mind when she booked this suite?" Ross asked. He bent his head forward, kissed the side of Frankie's neck.

Frankie purred, arched like a cat, purposely rubbing her delicious rump against his stirring rod, but inadvertently sloshing water out over the side of the tub. She chuckled softly. "Oh, it's definitely what she had in mind."

Ross filled his hands with water, then cupped her breasts. Her nipples pearled against his palms, tightened like ripe raspberries waiting to be eaten. He growled low in his throat, hungry again. As long as she stayed naked and room service never went on strike, he'd be perfectly content to spend the rest of his life right here. With her. "Then remind me to thank her when we get home," he whispered low.

Funny how he'd gone from dreading this trip to dreading that it would soon be over, he thought, once again struck by how perfectly their bodies melded together. Amazing the kind of attitude adjustment hours of mind-boggling, strength-sapping sex could help one put things into perspective.

For instance, they were both sore and tired

from hours of vigorous bed play. Soaking in the whirlpool tub to give a brief reprieve to their weary muscles had seemed like a nice way to still be intimate, but rest all the same. However, now that they were actually seated together in the tub, the hot water lapping around them, lulling their senses...her ass snugged right up against his groin and his hands full of plump, suckable breasts, Ross was having second thoughts.

About taking her again.

He slid one hand down her belly, parted the wet curls and dallied between her thighs until she was squirming against his hand and her breath was coming in short, static little puffs. For no apparent reason, she abruptly broke away.

"Out," she ordered, struggling from the tub. "Ross," she all but wailed. "You can't do this to me."

Confused, Ross stood and stepped out of the tub. Water sluiced down his body, puddled onto the fluffy rug beneath his feet.

"Without me being able to do it to you," she added slyly.

Then before he knew what she was about,

she wrapped her hand around his rod, dropped to her knees and proceeded to suck him *completely* into her mouth. His thighs quaked, his eyes rolled back in his head, and a low guttural groan which could only be described as ecstatic broke apart in his throat.

He looked down, watched her pulling him into her mouth, licking, sucking—*worshipping,* because she clearly loved having him in her mouth, the single most erotic turn-on for any guy—and honestly, he didn't think he'd ever seen anything so elementally sensual in his life. That carnal mouth, wrapped around his rod, her pink tongue lapping at him like a melting pop-sicle on the Fourth of July…

The only thing that could make it better was him doing it to her.

While she did it to him.

Less than five seconds later his mouth was fastened between her legs, his tongue working frantically against the swollen nub nestled at the crest of her sex.

Frankie whimpered around him, bucked beneath him, then pulled him even deeper into the hot cavern of her mouth. For every distracting, fantastic thing she did to him, he repaid it in kind. She cuddled his testicles, he slipped a finger deep inside her, hooked it around and found her G-spot.

Every muscle in her body went rigid, then she went *wild*. He felt her whimper around him, suck harder, then grab the twin muscles of his ass and hold him so that he couldn't pull away.

As if, Ross thought, bracing himself as his loins prepared to detonate. He stiffened his tongue, curled it until it snugly cradled her clit, then lapped even harder against her.

A nanosecond later, he felt her spasm around his finger, felt her nether lips quiver beneath his. The sweet nectar of her release hit his tongue and he savored every ounce of it, licked and licked until he'd feasted his fill.

Then he came.

Hard.

Though her body was still trembling, Frankie never missed a beat. She growled with pleasure, as though savoring a particularly tasty dessert. She licked, sucked, milked him until his vision blackened around the edges and his head grew too heavy to support with his own strength. He rolled over and let it drop to the floor.

Utterly spent, breathing heavily, Ross laughed and flung an arm over his forehead. "Frankie?"

She snuggled up beside him, pillowed her head against his chest. Her hair slithered over him, tickling his side, drawing a contented smile across his face. They were on the damned *bathroom floor*, and yet he couldn't find the energy to move. "Yes?"

"Do I have permission to die now?"

He felt her chuckle, the breeze of her sweet breath whisper across his nipple, and something light and warm inflated in his chest.

"No," she said, her voice low and foggy, "but if you help me get to the bed, I'll let you sleep."

"Done." He stood and, though he didn't have any idea where he found the wherewithal, he hoisted her slight frame into his arms and, very gallantly if he did say so himself considering that she was naked, hauled her into the other room and very gently deposited her onto the bed.

Ross turned off the light, slid in beside her,

then spooned her up firmly against him. Frankie settled against him, sighed contentedly and that soft sound wormed its way into his heart, seemed to lodge there just as firmly as she had.

He fell asleep with her breast in his hand, the soft, steady tune of her breathing in his ears…and the unmistakable knowledge that he'd landed smack-dab in the middle of the one thing he swore he'd never dip a toe into—love.

Game, set, match, indeed, he thought groggily…and she'd won.

11

New York City

IF SHE WOULD HAVE HAD even so much as five minutes to herself after her *heart-bone-brain* melting night with Ross, Frankie would have liked to think that she could have gotten her head on straight. That she might have been able to extricate him from her thoughts and ultimately her heart, but she sincerely doubted that would have been the case.

As it was, she'd never know, because whether he'd suspected that she'd backslide or not, Ross hadn't given her the opportunity to think about anything beyond having a good time with him.

They'd barely rolled out of bed this morning in time to make their flight to New York—Ross, damn his hide, had decided that a shared shower would expedite matters—then rather than proceeding directly to the baggage claim to pick up the mountain of luggage she bitterly regretted bringing, he'd convinced her to follow him into the men's room, where he'd proceeded to lift her skirt, nudge her panties aside and take her hard and fast against a bathroom door.

A scene from that frantic coupling materialized behind her lids, made her even warmer in places that kept a perpetual fever, or at least around him, she thought with a wry smile. Her belly vibrated, her sex sang and her breasts grew impossibly heavy with want. He'd treated her to a toe-curling orgasm a mere two hours ago, and yet here she stood listening to him extol the virtues of *swallowing vs. not,* miserably, wretchedly horny again.

He sent her a secret look hot enough to melt steel. "Trust me. There is absolutely nothing more erotic than having a woman swallow." He paused, let his gaze drift toward her mouth, wordlessly letting her know that he was reliving the moment she'd done it to him. "Aside from the fact that it makes a regular orgasm a *phenomenal* orgasm," he emphasized with a dramatic wincing shudder, "there's something utterly sexy about knowing that your partner was so into tasting you that she wanted more of you than just the main course—that she hung around for the dessert as well." A smile flirted with his unusually sexy mouth.

She could go for some dessert, Frankie thought vaguely as she let go a halting breath. In fact, Ross was looking particularly tasty today. He wore a dark green shirt which show-cased every muscle, bump and ridge of his impressive anatomy— -as well as made the most of those heavily fringed mega-hazel eyes—and a pair of casual khaki trousers which hugged the perfect curve of his mouth-watering ass and complimented his impossibly lean hips.

Convinced that he couldn't be perfect, Frankie had surveyed his body at length last night, but aside from a half-moon-shaped scar just below his elbow, she couldn't find a single flaw. And predictably, she'd decided that the scar didn't detract from the overall beauty of his magnificent frame, but rather added character.

Frankie's gaze slid to where Ross stood be-side her, to the curiously vulnerable side of his neck where his hair curled adorably behind his ear, and felt her heart perform a little pirouette. She let go a resigned breath and gave her head a futile, helpless shake.

She was a lost cause and she knew it.

After answering a couple more questions— "What's the best position for stimulating your G-spot?" and "Do guys respond to nipple stimulation as well?"—Frankie rounded off another astonishingly successful *CHiC* session, then officially called the gathering to a close. To her delight, every single meeting had continued to grow, and, as an added bonus, their Chicago to New York numbers had doubled.

Frankie would love to take complete credit for the success of the tour, but she knew better. Though he'd only been on the scene for a few days, her Duke of Desire had made one helluva impression. The majority of the attendants who were turning up at their sessions were people who'd either heard about his good looks or their super-sizzling chemistry. She shrugged mentally, snagged her purse from behind the podium. Either way, the bottom line was good for *CHiC*.

Though he probably wasn't going to like the idea, Frankie was going to suggest to Zora that he write a guest column for the magazine. He'd been too much of a success to simply vanish from the *CHiC* world after this promotional tour was over.

Ross pushed his hand into hers, threaded their fingers together, the tender gesture bringing another unexpected jolt of pleasure into her heart. He cocked his dark head toward hers and his eyes glinted with sexy humor. "Hungry?" he asked suggestively.

Frankie bit the inside of her cheek, fought the urge to smile. "Let me guess," she replied drolly. "You want to treat me to dessert?"

His eyes twinkled. "I'll even make it myself."

She grinned. She'd just bet he would, the wretch.

A woman she recognized with the PR firm hurried forward as they made their way offstage. "Ms. Salvaterra?"

Frankie paused. "Yes?"

"Several of the local affiliates would like to do a few quick interviews. Are you interested?"

Was she interested? In free national press? Hell, yes, she was interested. Excitement tickled every nerve ending and pushed a proud smile up her lips. Only by sheer force of will did she resist the urge to bounce on the balls of her feet. This was *fantastic*. Beyond fantastic, she decided, as the full ramifications of what this sort of exposure could do for *CHiC*, especially this early in the game.

Frankie looked expectantly at Ross who, for reasons she didn't understand, didn't appear to share her enthusiasm. A troubled frown knitted his brow and he seemed to be wrestling with some sort of weighty decision. "Do you mind?" she asked.

He hesitated. "Er…"

"Come on," she cajoled, squeezing his hand. "What's the problem? Do you have any idea how great this is? Do you know what it means?"

To her vast relief, he finally nodded bracingly and a curiously brittle smile moved into place. "You're right, of course. Let's do it."

Elated, Frankie grinned, pulled him down and planted a lingering kiss on his lips. A wash of hot fizzies started at her scalp and worked their way down. She lowered her voice to a more intimate level and shamelessly pressed her breast against his arm. "I'll be ready for dessert afterward," she promised.

Atlanta

"GOOD NEWS, ROSS. She's quit calling."

Ross's hand froze on the super-sized box of condoms he'd just snagged from the hotel gift shop shelf. "Completely?"

"Yeah." Charley laughed, his voice ringing with obvious relief. "Haven't heard a peep out of her since after ten last night. Which is good, because let me tell you, the last few messages she'd left were a little on the creepy side. She'd sounded more agitated, angry."

Ross felt a prickling of uncomfortable awareness hit the back of his neck. She'd been more agitated and angry and yet she'd stopped calling? He frowned warily. That didn't make any sense, and rather than boding well, Ross got the distinct impression that this news could be otherwise.

Yesterday he'd let Frankie jump to the incorrect assumption that he didn't want to do those interviews because he'd rather go back to their room and have sex—him feed her dessert—which actually wasn't an incorrect assumption once he really thought about it, Ross amended, momentarily sidetracked by the idea of putting himself firmly between her thighs. In fact, he'd prefer going back to the room and stretching her petite little body out on a bed to anything else.

But the reason Ross hadn't wanted to do those interviews didn't have anything to do with delayed sex—he hadn't wanted to risk the possibility that Amy would see him on the late-night news. And, he thought grimly, unfortunately, the timeline of her apparent return to sanity jived with his concerns.

If she'd watched the news, then that meant she knew exactly where he was, that there was no reason for her to keep frantically trying to run him to ground. The idea that she could have been in the crowd during their morning session made his coffee sour in his stomach, his insides involuntarily cramp with dread.

Up until this point, Ross had never really considered that she might be dangerous, but now the niggling notion took root and grew in the fertile field of his imagination. Ross gave his head a little shake to dislodge the idea. He was being dramatic, dammit, letting her get to him. Hell, the chances of her taking off from

New Orleans for Atlanta in the middle of the night were slim to none. Right? Right, he told himself.

Shaking the shadow of premonition off his shoulders, he asked Charley if he'd had any other messages. Just one from Tate, he'd learned before disconnecting, regarding the Maxwell account he hadn't given a second thought since the first night they'd started this trip.

At first Ross felt a little guilty for not getting any more done on it than he had, but then the self-righteous voice of reason had chimed in and made quick work of the regret.

Number one, Tate had given him the Maxwell account because he deserved it. It had merely been a tool to get him on board with this trip, Ross realized now, and due to the fact that he was a driven SOB, it had worked pathetically well. He'd been too easily manipulated, a fact that he'd need to think about at a later time.

Number two, the sole purpose of him being Frankie's Duke of Desire had been about getting them together. He felt a smile catch the corner of his mouth and tug. Given that they'd gone to so much trouble to hook them up, it seemed counterproductive to their purposes for Ross to actually work on something for Hatcher Advertising.

No, if Ross had to hazard a guess, the message from Tate had been more of a plea for information. Tate was evidently too proud to ask his wife if her plan had worked—he'd undoubtedly be eating crow, Ross imagined—and instead had wanted to pump him for information.

Ross walked to the counter and paid for the condoms, then began the return trek upstairs. While he knew he owed Tate and Zora a thanks, he wasn't feeling particularly charitable with the method they'd employed. They'd argue that the end justified the means, and who knew? They were probably right. But the high-handed way they'd bet on his and Frankie's future still didn't sit right with him.

Especially knowing what he knew now about her father.

Earlier in the week Ross had realized that Frankie had been hurt by someone, that her hard-edged sarcasm was a defense mechanism that she'd mastered out of self-preservation, but he'd had no idea that that person was her father, the one man that she should have been able to count on to never hurt her, to never let her down.

In the wee hours of the morning, Frankie had lain in his arms and, though he'd had to prod her for answers to his questions at first, she'd eventually shared the whole sordid tale. The haircut, the beatings, the infidelity and cruelty.

By the time she was finished, his body was atrophied with anger and the idea of tracking him down and beating the bloody hell out of him had taken on the pretty sheen of a shiny new toy.

Ross wanted to hurt him like he'd never wanted to hurt another person. He wanted to kick his ass for every infraction against Frankie, and even her mom who evidently was too co-dependent to think for herself. He wanted her to put her mercy into his hands, let *him* be *her* bully, his strength hers.

In short, he wanted to take care of her.

He wanted to be everything to her that no other man had ever been. Her hero, her friend, her confidant and her champion. He wanted to right every wrong, make up for every slight. He could do it, Ross thought. He could do it if it meant he could be hers.

The idea of belonging to another person—of permanently attaching himself to one—had never been a notion that Ross had entertained—in fact, it had always been one that he staunchly avoided—and, though it gave him more than a little pause now, the idea of *not* belonging to her somehow seemed far worse.

Ross imagined that it was a little too early in their relationship to be thinking about a permanent attachment, but when he thought about Frankie—pictured himself five, even ten years from now—he couldn't see himself without her. The image wouldn't gel, wouldn't compute and, frankly, even trying to make it made his belly chill with a sort of panicked dread.

He loved her, Ross thought simply.

He'd known from the first instant that he laid eyes on her that she was different, that she was special. She was the ultimate trophy, *his* ultimate prize.

And he wouldn't be satisfied until he made her irrevocably, the till-death-do-us-part kind of his.

Ross slipped into their room, smiled when he caught the sound of running water. So she was in the shower. That was as good a place as any to plead his case, Ross thought with a wicked smile, shedding clothes as he went. Anticipation sent a flash of heat straight to his loins. After all, he could negotiate better when she was naked.

Scented steam billowed around him as he strolled into the large glamour bath. He fished a condom out of the box, tore into the foil packet with his teeth.

"Want some company?" he called. He drew the curtain back, then staggered in shock at the woman standing there. His eyes widened.

"As a matter of fact, I do," she said, her lips curled into a hard smile. "You've been avoiding me, haven't you, Ross?"

For all intents and purposes the shrieking music from the Amityville horror films might as well have materialized right there in the bathroom with him.

Amy.

Panic the likes of which he'd never known ricocheted through his chest, pumping his heartrate into prestroke level. *Dear God,* Ross thought as nausea clawed its way up the back of his throat, *where was Frankie?*

He swallowed, resisted the immediate urge to drag her forcibly out of the shower. Before he did anything, he had to know that… That he hadn't let this *nut* do anything to hurt Frankie. Dammit, he'd been so stupid. So freakin' stupid. He should have told her, Ross thought. The idea that his ego had possibly resulted in her tragedy made him want to vomit.

With effort, he cleared his unbelievably tight throat. "Where's Frankie?"

Amy laughed. "Don't worry. I got rid of her."

Ross died a thousand deaths in that instant. He sagged against the wall. "What?"

"She's in the lobby bar meeting a reporter who's never going to show," she said. "I doubt she's as patient as me, though." Her eyes narrowed fractionally. "I've been waiting for weeks to hear from you. Why didn't you call me back?" she demanded. "Why wouldn't you answer my calls? Do you have any idea how hard I've been trying to get in touch with you?" Her voice climbed with every question and her gaze took on a slightly manic look.

Now that he knew Frankie was okay, Ross felt some of the strength seep back into his limbs, undoubtedly enhanced by the anger now chugging speedily through his veins. "Yes, I do, Amy," Ross replied firmly lest there be any mistake, "because I've been trying equally hard to *avoid* you." He pulled in a ragged breath, tried and failed to maintain patience. *"We aren't a couple. We were never a couple. We are not dating anymore."*

She looked like he'd slapped her, like he'd never told her these things before. It was utterly mind-boggling. "You— You can't mean that," she breathed, seemingly crushed. "You love me." Her voice was small, almost childlike. "I know you do." She moved toward him, wrapped her arms around his neck.

Repulsed, Ross pulled back, but she stubbornly clung to him. "No, I don't," he said tightly, trying to shrug her off without hurting her. He swore hotly. "Amy, let go. You… You need help," he told her. And she did. She was clearly unbalanced. How in the hell had he missed a psychosis of this proportion, he wondered, trying once again to tug her arms from around his neck.

Amy suddenly stilled. Ross looked down and

caught the delighted look on her face as she gazed at something over his left shoulder. "Look, baby," she said. "We've got company."

Oh, Christ. Not this, Ross thought, his stomach seizing. Anything but this. The floor seemed to tilt beneath his feet. He twisted around, Amy still fastened like a barnacle against his naked body.

Frankie stood frozen in the doorway, her face white. A flash of stark, devastating pain lit her dark brown eyes before a shutter moved into place. Her mouth formed a familiar mocking smile. "Sorry to interrupt," she said, then turned abruptly on her heel and walked out.

Ross swore hotly, stopped being the gentleman and shoved Amy off of him. He knew he hadn't hurt her, but she cried out all the same. "Ross!" she shrieked. "Let her go."

His pulse roaring in his ears, Ross hurried after her. "Frankie, wait! It's not what you— I know it looks—" Oh, hell, he couldn't even finish the explanation, it was so damned clichéd.

She never missed a step and he, being naked, dammit, couldn't follow her out into the hall. "Wait! Please!" Oh, shit. Shit. Shit. Shit. He leaned out into the hall as far as he could go. "For the love of God, woman, would you please just stop and listen to me?"

"You can die now," she called without so much as a backward glance, her voice flat and emotionless, as though she'd predicted this very end.

A bundle of frustration and energy, Ross dropped into a squat, then vaulted back up and plowed his fingers through his hair. He paced and swore, then slammed his fist into the wall, knocking a hole the size of a cup saucer into the Sheetrock.

"Temper, temper," Amy chided with a bizarre-sounding giggle. "You'll have to pay for that."

Eyes narrowed. Ross turned slowly to face her. She flinched, presumably from his black-ened expression. *"Get out,"* he said deliberately. *"Get out and never come near me again."*

Her eyes rounded. "You don't mean that."

Oh, but he did. "I'm going to give you to the count of three to leave," Ross told her, his voice hard and throbbing with anger. "If you don't— or if you ever contact me in any shape, form, or fashion again—I'm going to call the police and press charges."

"But—"

He let go a furious breath and shook his head. "One…"

"But, Ross—"

He took a threatening step forward. "Two…"

She squealed, bent and gathered her clothes, and with one longing look back at him, she hurried from the room.

He sank to the end of the bed and pushed a shaky hand through his hair. Allowed himself a moment to pull it together, then he got up, dressed and quickly went downstairs.

His hummingbird was fast—if he didn't catch her before she left, he'd have a helluva time of it once she'd made it to her nest.

You can die now, she'd said, and Ross knew a part of him would if he lost her.

12

IF HER FATHER had ever taught her one good thing it was being able to turn pain—a devastating, completely unproductive emotion—into fury, a good therapeutic alternative with the added bonus of providing one with a purpose.

Take now for instance. Instead of breaking down in Atlanta, securing another room in a different hotel, and hiding away to lick her wounds in secret, Frankie had arranged for the hotel to ship her things to her house and had rented a car. She was now somewhere between Tuscaloosa and New Orleans and with each mile she put between them the more numb she became.

Numb, for obvious reasons, was good.

Being numb meant she couldn't feel the gaping hole in her chest, or the prickly, burning sensation behind her eyes, or the hot splashes of liquid emotion currently trekking down her cheeks.

She wasn't crying, she wasn't hurt, and the muffin she'd had for breakfast had given her indigestion.

She would be fine. She was a hummingbird, dammit, fragile but strong and able to withstand anything life threw at her. If she could survive a boot-camp childhood with Frank Salvaterra, she could survive *anything* and she would survive this.

She would.

While other women might have moaned and groaned and lamented about what might have been, Frankie wouldn't allow herself to indulge in any such behavior because she'd known when she'd given herself to him that she'd get hurt, had known from the beginning—from the first instant she'd laid eyes on him—that he'd break her heart.

Crying was futile.

Even so, the knowing didn't lessen the pain, and she honestly hadn't known when she'd made the decision to sleep with him that the price of her pleasure would be a sensation akin to having her guts yanked from her belly and her heart filleted. If she had, she'd have most likely stuck with her vibrator and saved herself the trouble.

More than anything, she just felt like a fool and she absolutely would not allow Ross to make a wreck of her. She couldn't permit it. She wouldn't become some miserable fishwife who continually hosted her own pity party, and she damned sure wouldn't let him know that she'd believed—even for one minute—that she'd thought he was different. Another jagged piece of her heart crumbled away, causing her to catch her breath.

Men were men, and just because Ross had seemed like the genuine article, just because he'd bought her the first thoughtful gift she'd received in years and had decked her father for her didn't mean that he was special.

Furthermore, just because she'd occasionally caught him looking at her with something which too closely resembled the affection she continually starved for, well… Her lips twisted with bitter humor. Clearly she'd been wrong.

Her eyes hadn't lied.

Ross had been standing in the bathroom with another woman. They'd both been naked. Thanks to her father, she had too much experience with infidelity to not realize it when she saw it. It didn't take a rocket scientist to make the deduction that she'd interrupted something, that the "reporter" incident had been a sham that one or both of them had planned.

The irony was, ordinarily she would have sat for at least another hour and waited for the so-called reporter to show—news didn't adhere to a time schedule and, in her experience in dealing with reporters, as a rule they were generally late.

Here's where the irony part came in. The idea of being away from Ross, even for another hour, had been too much to bear, so she'd decided to stand up the reporter and go back to him.

Bastard, she thought, her throat tightening painfully.

Granted, he'd seemed more than a bit distraught. Frankie had seen the panicked expression in those hurtfully beautiful eyes, had seen a litany of curses form on his lips. She hadn't heard them—at the time she hadn't been able to hear anything above the roaring in her ears.

Furthermore, he'd seemed particularly determined to explain himself—not the typical behavior of a man who'd been caught doing something wrong, she had to admit—and she'd gotten the distinct impression that, had he had so much as a tissue to cover his dick, he would have hied off down the hall after her.

In addition, the careless way he shrugged the woman off of him when she'd seen them together had suggested that Ms. Naked wasn't anyone special to him. But then, that was probably the point, eh?

They were all interchangeable.

But not her. She wouldn't be.

Not for him, not for anybody. The bitch could have him, Frankie thought. She'd keep her self-respect, thank you very much.

A cold comfort, she thought as another painful ache swelled in her chest, but it was better than nothing.

ROSS SHOT TO HIS FEET, patiently waited for the older gentleman in front of him to drag his attaché down from the overhead compartment. Impatience strummed across his nerves, made his fingers flex and bite into his palms.

He'd spent the better part of three hours looking for Frankie, and by the time he'd found out that she'd arranged to have her considerable luggage shipped home and had rented a car, he'd already missed the last direct flight out of Atlanta to New Orleans.

Ideally, he would have liked to have beaten her home, to have intercepted her before she arrived at her nest, but naturally, when something as important as his future was on the line, he thought darkly, his luck hadn't held out.

He'd ended up taking a sooner flight with a connection in Cincinnati, and from there things had only worsened. Bad weather in Ohio had kept planes grounded for an additional three hours, so the flight that should have put him there just slightly ahead of her had ended up putting him several hours behind her.

He growled, irritated beyond his endurance.

The older man in front of him finally managed to drag his small bag down, and the line of people clogging the aisle of the plane slowly dispersed. Ross hit the concourse at a fast jog, then wasted precious moments waiting for his luggage to finally emerge from the baggage carousel.

Beyond that, though, he made up valuable time and soon he found himself roaring into her drive. Her Thunderbird sat beneath the carport and another smaller vehicle, presumably the rental she'd driven all the way home, was pulled in behind it. A touch of the hood confirmed that she'd been home for a while—it was cool. Which meant she'd not only had the seven-plus hour drive home to wrap her mind around lots of wrong-headed little ideas, but another hour or so in her sanctuary to strengthen her resolve.

Not good, he decided.

Ross mounted the steps two at a time and knocked on her door. "Frankie?" he called. "Come on, I know you're home."

A curtain fluttered to his left and he hurried over there, tapped at the window. "I have to talk to you, dammit," Ross told her.

"Go away."

A-ha. A response. "I'm not leaving. I have to talk to you. You can't just walk off without giving me a chance to explain."

"What makes you think I'm interested—*that I even care*—about your explanations?" she demanded with an infuriating chuckle. "It's that big head again," she told him. "It gets you into trouble every time."

So that was how she intended to play it, Ross thought, a black haze swimming before his eyes, as though the past week together had meant nothing. That he'd just been a convenient distraction that she could easily dismiss once they were home?

Oh, how galling. If he wasn't in love with her, he'd undoubtedly throttle the living hell out of her.

"I'm not going to let you do this," he told her, lead in his voice. "I will stand out here all night if I have to. I will air every sordid piece of my dirty laundry right here in front of your neighbors if that's what you want."

"I don't want anything from you, Ross," she said wearily. "I thought I made that plain."

He was getting damned tired of talking through the door. He gestured wildly. "Would you please either let me in or come outside?"

"No. Go home." She laughed again, that

mocking sound that he'd grown so accustomed to, but hadn't heard in days. It ripped him up, cut him to the quick more than anything else she could have done because it meant that they were back at square one. "You're making a fool of yourself."

Ross smirked, leaned wearily against her door. "Actually, that's what I had been trying to avoid, dammit." He blew out a breath. "That woman you saw in our room has been…harassing me for weeks." He still couldn't bring himself to call her a stalker. "She's the one who's been sending me packages, calling me over and over, writing me letters, showing up at my house." He pushed off from the door, moved to peek into the window and saw Frankie's silhouette standing curiously still next to her front door.

"*She's* why I didn't want to do the interviews in New York—I was afraid she'd find me." He tilted his head back, laughed grimly. "And she did. She placed the call to our room, feigned being a reporter to lure you out, then tricked housekeeping into letting her into the room." He blew out a breath. "When I came in, I thought it was *you* in the shower, dammit. I—I didn't know it was her."

Another peek into the window confirmed that she'd moved closer and seemed to be listening.

"I took off my clothes in anticipation of joining you, dammit, and ended up with friggin' Glenn Close instead." Another grim laugh echoed past his teeth. "Lemme tell you, it was quite a shock." Ross toed at a loose board on the porch, reached up and massaged his temples, exhaled another mighty breath.

"When you walked in I was trying to get her off me, *not* get her into bed, Frankie," Ross said wearily. "You're the only woman I'm interested in sleeping with. Ever again," he added for good measure.

He heard her lock tumble back, watched the door open and a rebellious sprout of hope took root in his icy chest.

She didn't open the screen door, but rather stood there, unblinking at him. Her beautiful dark eyes were puffy and bloodshot, suggesting that she'd been crying, and fatigue lined every muscle of her body. More than anything, Ross wanted to lessen the distance between them, hold her and never let go. But he knew better. Hummingbirds were one of the only species that could fly backward and the last thing he wanted to do was give her any reason to retreat.

She crossed her arms over her chest. Her voice, when she spoke, was measured and even. "Are you telling me that you have a stalker?"

He flinched at the term, readied his mouth for a comeback, but stopped short when his cell vibrated at his waist. *Shit,* Ross thought. *Not now.* He checked the display. "It's Charley," he told her with an apologetic shrug. "I've got to get it." Ross answered the call. "What's up, Charley?"

Charley's panic-ridden voice came breathlessly across the line and what he had to say made every bit of the air evacuate Ross's own lungs. "Call the police. I'll be right there."

"Yes, that's exactly what I'm telling you," Ross told her, his voice throbbing with angry fear, his heart squeezing with fury and panic. "I have a stalker...and the bitch just nabbed my dog."

FRANKIE inhaled sharply. "What?"

Ross retreated down the steps. "She's got Otis," he called. "Charley let him out in the backyard to go to the bathroom, rinsed his water bowl with the hose, and when he turned around, he saw her bolting away with my damned dog. Sorry," he sighed. "I've got to go."

"Do you want me to come with you?"

His expression was heart-wrenchingly relieved. "Yes, I'd like that very much."

Frankie snagged her keys from the hook by the door, twisted the lock and pulled it closed, then hurried down the steps. She slid into the passenger seat, and before she could get the buckle fastened across her lap Ross had shot out of the drive.

"Have you contacted the police in the past about this woman?"

"No."

She knew he was worried about Otis, so rather than scream at him—her first inclination—Frankie made a valiant effort to keep her voice level. "Why not?"

He negotiated a turn, sped up. The dash lights illuminated his grim profile, the achingly familiar shape of his jaw, those sexy-as-sin lips. "For the same reason I didn't want to tell you—it's embarrassing."

Frankie's mouth dropped open and she swiveled to face him. Keeping her voice level was no longer an option. "Embarrassing?" she repeated shrilly. "That's why you've put me through this hell? Why I thought *the one guy* I'd ever believed in—that I ever trusted—was a two-timing, scum-sucking jerk? Why Otis has been dog-napped by some jilted crazy who doesn't know when to take no for an answer?"

A muscle flexed in his tense jaw. "In hindsight, it does seem rather stupid."

"It's more that stupid, Ross," she huffed, absolutely stunned at his ignorance. "It's reckless and irresponsible, not to mention just plain dumb."

"Ah, well," he sighed, sending her a somewhat droll smile. "This must mean that we've made up, otherwise you wouldn't be insulting me again."

Frankie felt her lips twitch. Leave it to Ross to go directly to the heart of the matter. "You should have told me."

Tires squealed as he made the turn onto his street. "You would have made fun."

That was fair, Frankie conceded. "I probably would have at first, but as soon as I realized the gravity of the situation, I would have done the smart thing and advised you to go to the police," she said pointedly.

"See," Ross sighed resignedly. "This is precisely why I love you. You're such a sweet, modest girl, with few opinions and the rare inclination to share them." Blue lights flashed in the distance, presumably at his house. "Good, they're here already," Ross said, apparently not realizing that he'd just dropped a mini-bomb onto her world. "Charley must have called the police before he called me," he murmured distractedly.

He pulled to a short stop, shifted into Park, then jumped out of the car. Still shell-shocked, Frankie followed him. Ross hurried over to a thin, lanky guy with an unfortunate sense of style. Charley, she imagined. A couple of uniformed officers stood with him.

"Well?" Ross asked.

Seemingly miserable, Charley hung his head. "I just gave them the information. I pulled her address off of one of those letters she'd sent, gave that to them, and I gave them a description of the car she was driving." His expression turned anguished. "Ross, I—"

"It's not your fault, Charley," Ross said firmly. Though he was clearly upset over Otis, he still had the presence of mind to make sure that Charley didn't blame himself. Ross shook his head. "This is my fault. I just didn't realize…" He swore, then turned to one of the officers. "What now?" he asked.

"We've radioed another car and they're looking now. As soon as we hear something we'll let you know. Luckily we were in the area when the call came in, and I doubt that she's going to get very far."

Ross plunged his hands into his hair, slicking it back away from his forehead. He let go a long breath and nodded. Frankie's heart broke for him. She knew that he loved the dog. She'd listened to him tell Charley repeatedly to take care of him. Knew that he could have just as easily boarded him at one of the veterinary clinics, but had opted for in-home care to prevent Otis from having to leave. That loyalty thing again, Frankie thought with a smile that was both fond and sad.

"I'm so sorry, Ross," Charley repeated, his shoulders rounded beneath a weight of guilt. Seemingly puzzled, he shook his head. "I still don't know how she did it. How did she get in through that back gate? It was locked."

Ross grimaced. "That didn't keep her from getting into the house," he said. "Locks aren't much of a deterrent to this woman."

Frankie's eyes widened and the officers shared a significant look. "She's broken into your house?" she asked, her voice once again skirting the edge of hysterical.

He nodded once. "I changed the locks, though, and she never did it again."

One of the officers frowned. "Has this woman been bothering you, sir?"

Ross rubbed the back of his neck, hedging. "Yeah, I guess you could call it that."

When it was evident that Ross was uncomfortable elaborating, Frankie ticked off every one of the woman's offenses. "She needs help," she said matter-of-factly. "And—" Her gaze slid to Ross. "He needs a restraining order."

The officer nodded. "You'll be pressing charges, of course?"

"Yes, he will," Frankie piped up. "For everything. Breaking and entering, stalking, harassment and the dog-napping."

Ross shot her a look, chewed the corner of his smile. "Taking care of me, are you?"

She harrumphed under her breath, rolled her eyes. "Evidently somebody needs to. I can't believe you let yourself get bullied by a girl. And a little one at that. Hell, I could've taken her."

"You bully me," he pointed out.

"No," she replied levelly. "I love you. There's a difference."

Frankie swallowed a gasp and her gaze flew to his when she realized what she'd just said. Luckily a question from one of the officers prevented her from having to explain herself.

"You got her address from letters, you say?" he asked.

Charley nodded.

The officer turned to Ross. "We'll need those, as well as any other evidence to help your case."

"I've thrown several of them away, but she's sent more."

"Would you mind getting those together?" he asked. "At this point, all we can do is wait."

Though he looked like he'd rather stay outside and wait for word with them, Ross capitulated.

Charley jerked his thumb over his shoulder toward his house. "I'm gonna head on home, Ross. Would you mind letting me know as soon as you hear something?"

"Sure. I'll call you."

Looking grim but determined and just a wee bit lost, Ross gestured for her to follow him and strode into the house.

While he hurried around the house gathering up letters, gifts and the tape from his answering machine, Frankie passed the time by wandering around his den. She inspected photographs, his DVD and CD collection, but eventually ended up in front of his impressive trophy collection.

Tee-ball, football, baseball, basketball, soccer. MVP, All-County, All-State, Best Defensive Player, Best Offensive Player, game balls and other memorabilia.

Hell, Frankie thought, amazed, was there a sport he hadn't played? There were dozens of trophies for each sport, a gold and plastic record of his early youth through his late teens.

Laden with his evidence, Ross walked back through the living room. He slowed when he saw her, then came to a cautious stop. "Looking at my Wall of Futility?" he asked with what sounded like a forced laugh.

Frankie frowned. "Wall of Futility?"

Ross set everything aside and came to stand beside her. His gaze roved over the wall, lingered over particular trophies. He picked up a game ball and a fond laugh bubbled up his throat, presumably from a happy memory. "This," he said with a long sigh, "is my wall of futility because, as a boy, I thought that the more time I spent on a sports field, the longer my parents would stay married. The less they would fight, the happier they would be." He said it matter-of-factly, as though it wasn't a source of pain, that it was, in fact, kind of funny. "So long as I was playing—and playing well," he added. "Everything was fine."

Frankie felt a peculiar sort of horror move through her. She looked at the wall again, the sheer volume of trophies, and the amount of time and work he'd devoted to each…and her heart broke for the little boy he'd been—the tough little overachiever desperately trying to keep his family together. She blinked back tears.

"It worked, too," Ross told her, his voice deceptively light. "Right up until my senior year when a torn ACL put me out of the game permanently." He shook his head. "Lost my scholarship. Mom and Dad split." Another forced laugh sounded. "Bad year."

"Oh, Ross," Frankie sighed. "I'm so sorry."

"Don't be," he said. "I'm not. I played for them, not for myself. In retrospect, it was the best thing that ever happened to me."

"Still…"

His gaze shifted past her shoulder, sharpened and he bolted into action. "Another cruiser just pulled up," he said abruptly. "Let's go."

Ross was almost to the door before she could make the connection. She grabbed the letters and other evidence that Ross had gathered, then forgotten, and hurried after him.

"He's got him," one of the officers called and they loped down the front steps.

Ross let go a visible sigh, wilted with relief, and the tension which had kept him rigid for the past hour seemed to melt right out of his shoulders.

Seeing his master, Otis barked, planted his little paws on the car window as they rolled to a stop. The officer driving the car reached across and opened the front door, letting the dog hop down. The woman, Amy, if memory served, Frankie thought, sat in the back.

"Careful," the officer called. "He's a little tipsy." He gave a baffled laugh. "Apparently, she lured him to the back gate with a beer."

True enough, a very obviously trashed Otis weaved and wobbled from side to side as he hurried on unsteady legs toward Ross.

Smiling wide, Ross squatted down to greet him, tousled the dog's big floppy ears. "Hey, there, buddy," he chuckled fondly. "What are you doing fallin' off the wagon, huh? You know better than to hit the hard stuff."

"Are you coming in tonight to fill out that paperwork we talked about?" the one officer asked.

Still patting the dog, Ross looked up and winced. "Can it keep until tomorrow? I'm pretty beat."

"Yeah," he said, moving toward the patrol car. Frankie intercepted him, handed him the evidence she'd brought outside. "But I wouldn't let it go any longer than that."

"I won't."

The rest of the officers loaded up and prepared to depart. "G'night, then. You folks have a nice evening."

"Sure."

Frankie bent down and rubbed Otis's knobby head, unsure of what to say now that they were alone.

"Is it true?" he asked, seemingly as an afterthought.

Confused, Frankie looked up and her gaze tangled with his. "Is what true?"

"What you said. About loving me." He cleared his throat. "Do you love me?"

Truth for truth, Frankie thought. She slowly pushed herself to her feet, took a step closer to him. "I do."

His gaze softened and just the smallest hint of masculine pride clung to his ever-widening smile.

"Was it true when you said it to me?" she asked, a little bit more belligerently than she probably should have considering this was supposed to be a tender moment. But hell, it was rude of him to stand there and bask in the glow of her love while leaving her shivering in the cold waiting for confirmation of his.

Ross chuckled softly, tugged her to him. Her body came up flush against his, a perfect fit that eased a slow, satisfied sigh from her lungs. "Yes, Frankie, I love you." He bent and kissed the tip of her nose. "I love the way you argue with me, the way you roll your eyes when I do something ignorant. I love the way your lips tremble when you're trying not to laugh, and the sweet curve of your cheek when you cock your head just so. I love the way you always swirl your straw around your drink before you take a sip, and I love the way your hair feels sliding over my chest and the adorable mewls of pleasure you make when I'm deep inside you." He sighed softly and that gorgeous gaze searched hers "But most of all, I love the way I feel when I'm with you." He brushed his lips over hers lightly. "Now do you want to throw the ball, or is it okay for me to score?"

Joy bolted through her, tickled every cell in her body, forcing a somewhat tearful laugh up her throat. "You can score," she told him.

Chuckling softly, he slung his arm around her

shoulders and nudged her toward the house. "Good… And if you'll trust me, I'll see to it *we* both score." He jiggled the dog's leash. "Come on, Otis, you big sot. You can sleep it off at the foot of the bed while I make love to my future wife."

Frankie stumbled. "Future wife?" she parroted.

"Sure," Ross said. "Aren't we getting married?"

"I don't know," Frankie said tightly, irritation running neck and neck with the joy of this moment. "You haven't asked me to marry you."

Ross mounted the steps. "I just thought it was a foregone conclusion." He pulled a baffled shrug. "People who love each other get married."

"People who love each other *ask*," she said through gritted teeth. "They don't *assume*."

She caught the faintest quiver of his lips right before he dropped down on one knee. "If you're willing to overlook the fact that I don't have a ring, I'll overlook the fact that you aren't a virgin."

She couldn't help it. Laughing, she whacked him. "Ross," she chided, outraged.

Still on one knee, he struggled to pull his smile in line. "Sorry," he said with false contrition.

Then every bit of the humor vanished from his compelling gaze and the depth of feeling and emotion that took its place practically knocked the breath out of her. "Francesca Grace Salvaterra, will you do me the honor of becoming my wife?"

Frankie felt a tear slip down her cheek and she nodded jerkily.

A wide smile broke across Ross's face and he stood, then framed her face and fastened his mouth onto hers. When he finally drew back his breathing was labored and a definite bulge nudged her belly.

Frankie purposely licked her lips, threaded her fingers through his and led him inside. "I'm ready for dessert."

"Game, set, match," Ross sighed happily.

Epilogue

One month later...

"I DUNNO, MAN," Tate teased. "I think you may have missed your calling."

Frankie's delectable Duke of Desire just shook his head, refusing to be baited. Which was just as well, Frankie thought, because she was the only person who was permitted to bait, annoy or otherwise provoke her fiancé.

"Stop needling him, Tate," Zora instructed. "Ross's post-launch article has been a huge hit." She let go a careful breath and looked hopefully at Ross. "So huge in fact that I'd really like him to consider maybe writing a feature to coincide with Frankie's weekly once a month. He's made your wife a lot of money."

"Yeah, well," Tate argued. "He's making Maxwell Commodities a lot of money, too."

Frankie sipped her Blue Monkey Margarita and listened with a half smile curling her lips. Tate and Zora had been fighting over Ross—and who ultimately got them together—like a dog over a bone for the past month. It was funny, really, the way that everything had worked out. She and Ross had settled into domestic bliss with virtually no problems, and whatever minor grievances occurred were usually settled in the neutral territory of the bedroom.

She gazed around the room and a contented peace settled over her shoulders like a comfortable old blanket. It was hard to believe that a little over a year ago she, Zora, April and Carrie had sat in this very pub and hammered out the idea of the *Chicks-In-Charge* organization, that the pro-women's group would have made such an impact on each of their lives as well as thousands of others' across America. Since its inception she and Zora had both found their callings, their soul mates, and she could only hope that April and Carrie would be so lucky as well. Which reminded her…

"Carrie's not going to make it?" Frankie asked.

Zora shook her head. "Martin's being a bastard again. She's working late."

Frankie scowled. Something needed to be done about him, she thought. Carrie was the best chef this side of the Mississippi, and had the prestigious advantage of working at New Orleans' best restaurant. The problem was the world's biggest bastard owned it. Supposedly *Let's Cook, New Orleans!* was looking at Carrie as a possible host, but so far nothing had come of it. For her friend's sake, she hoped something did soon.

Zora's gaze sharpened and she cocked her head to one side. "At least April made it," she said as the woman in question fought the crowd through the bar. A small frown emerged between her eyebrows and she shot Frankie a significant look. "Any news with her *situation?*" she asked.

Frankie shook her head. "No, not exactly. She's still…suffering." With a sly smile that only Zora would understand, Frankie leaned closer and imparted an interesting observation she'd just noticed. "But if you'll look down at the end of the bar, you'll notice a certain someone with legendary abilities staring a hot hole through our mutual friend."

Ben Hayes, whom she'd rarely seen at the Blue Monkey had begun to make regular visits to their out of the way little pub, and those visits usually coincided with the *Chicks-In-Charge* board meetings. A coincidence? She thought not.

It would be interesting to see just what happened between those two, Frankie thought. The heat was definitely there.

Ross squeezed her hand, and those kaleidoscope eyes of his regarded her with shrewd amusement. "I know that expression," he said, eyes twinkling. "That's the *mayhem* face." He quirked a brow. "What gives?"

"Nothing," Frankie said with a mysterious little smile she knew would drive him nuts. She swirled her straw around her drink. "Nothing at all."

But if April were lucky, Ben Hayes would give her that orgasm she needed.

If you enjoyed what you just read,
then we've got an offer you can't resist!

Take 2 bestselling
love stories FREE!

Plus get a FREE surprise gift!

eHARLEQUIN.com

The Ultimate Destination for Women's Fiction

Calling all aspiring writers!
Learn to craft the perfect romance novel with our useful tips and tools:

- Take advantage of our **Romance Novel Critique Service** for detailed advice from romance professionals.

- Use our **message boards** to connect with writers, published authors and editors.

- Enter our **Writing Round Robin—** you could be published online!

- Learn many tools of the writer's trade from editors and authors in our **On Writing** section!

- **Writing guidelines** for Harlequin or Silhouette novels—what our editors *really* look for.

Learn more about romance writing from the experts— visit www.eHarlequin.com today!

An Invitation for Love

Find a special way to invite your guy into your Harlequin Moment. Letting him know you're looking for a little romance will help put his mind on the same page as yours. In fact, if you do it right, he won't be able to stop thinking about you until he sees you again!

Send him a long-stemmed rose tied to an invitation that leaves a lot up to the imagination.

♥

Autograph a favorite photo of you and tape it on the appointed day in his day planner. Block out the hours he'll be spending with you.

♥

Send him a local map and put an *X* on the place you want him to meet you. Write: "I'm lost without you. Come find me. Tonight at 8." Use magazine cutouts and photographs to paste images of romance and the two of you all over the map.

♥

Send him something personal that he'll recognize as yours to his office. Write: "If found, please return. Owner offers reward to anyone returning item by 7:30 on Saturday night." Don't sign the card.

Harlequin on Location

hot tips

Wherever your dream date location,
pick a setting and a time that won't be
interrupted by your daily responsibilities.
This is a special time together. Here are
a few hopelessly romantic settings to
inspire you—they might as well be ripped
right out of a Harlequin romance novel!

Bad weather can be so good.

Take a walk together after a fresh snowfall or when it's just stopped raining. Pick a snowball (or a puddle) fight, and see how long it takes to get each other soaked to the bone. Then enjoy drying off in front of a fire, or perhaps surrounded by lots and lots of candles with yummy hot chocolate to warm things up.

Candlelight dinner for two...in the bedroom.

Romantic music and candles will instantly transform the place you sleep into a cozy little love nest, perfect for nibbling. Why not lay down a blanket and open a picnic basket at the foot of your bed? Or set a beautiful table with your finest dishes and glowing candles to set the mood. Either way, a little bubbly and lots of light finger foods will make this a meal to remember.

A Wild and Crazy Weeknight.

Do something unpredictable...on a weeknight straight from work. Go to an art opening, a farm-team baseball game, the local playhouse, a book signing by an author or a jazz club—anything but the humdrum blockbuster movie. There's something very romantic about being a little wild and crazy—or at least out of the ordinary—that will bring out the flirt in both of you. And you won't be able to resist thinking about each other in anticipation of your hot date...or telling everyone the day after.

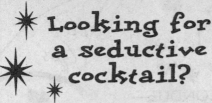

Looking for a seductive cocktail?

hot tips

Try **Ero-Desiac—**
a dazzling martini

With its warm apricot walls yet cool atmosphere, Verlaine is quickly becoming one of New York's hottest nightspots. Verlaine created a light, subtle yet seductive martini for Harlequin: the Ero-Desiac. Sake warms the heart and soul, while jasmine and passion fruit ignite the senses....

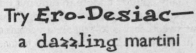

The Ero-Desiac

Combine vodka, sake, passion fruit puree and jasmine tea. Mix and shake. Strain into a martini glass, then rest pomegranate syrup on the edge of the martini glass and drizzle the syrup down the inside of the glass.

Are you a ❤ chocolate lover?

Try WALDORF ❤ ❤ CHOCOLATE FONDUE— a true chocolate decadence

While many couples choose to dine out on Valentine's Day, one of the most romantic things you can do for your sweetheart is to prepare an elegant meal—right in the comfort of your own home.

Harlequin asked John Doherty, executive chef at the Waldorf-Astoria Hotel in New York City, for his recipe for seduction—the famous Waldorf Chocolate Fondue....

WALDORF CHOCOLATE FONDUE
Serves 6-8

2 cups water
½ cup corn syrup
1 cup sugar
8 oz dark bitter chocolate, chopped
1 pound cake (can be purchased in supermarket)
2–3 cups assorted berries
2 cups pineapple
½ cup peanut brittle

Bring water, corn syrup and sugar to a boil in a medium-size pot. Turn off the heat and add the chopped chocolate. Strain and pour into fondue pot. Cut cake and fruit into cubes and 1-inch pieces. Place fondue pot in the center of a serving plate, arrange cake, fruit and peanut brittle around pot. Serve with forks.